TWO TREES

Robert Ingleson

MINERVA PRESS
MONTREUX LONDON WASHINGTON

TWO TREES
Copyright © Robert Ingleson 1997

ISBN 1 85863 963 8

First Published 1997 by
MINERVA PRESS
195 Knightsbridge
London SW7 1RE

Printed in Great Britain for Minerva Press

TWO TREES

Contents

Foreword

This is the story of two trees, told from three perspectives. First from a historical perspective. Second from the perspective of the owner of one of the trees and third from the perspective of the owner of the other tree.

The story spans the period of history from the start of time to the death and resurrection of Christ. It is a fictional account of this truly historical time. I write from a Christian viewpoint although I do not claim any doctrinal accuracy in what is represented. It is a journey of the imagination, entirely fictitious. If you as an individual perceive some spiritual truth within these pages, then it is an added bonus. The intention is not necessarily to represent truth but to represent history from alternative points of view and so stimulate your thinking and imagination. How closely my imagination coupled with yours matches the real truth is something that only you can decide, and ultimately God will judge.

And so there are two trees. Family trees actually. One is alive and one is dead. Of course, it is difficult at first glance to tell which is which. A little like taking an evergreen in winter, chopping it down at ground level and planting the stub next to an apple tree. The evergreen is dead. Finished. It looks very much alive but it is dead, within a few weeks it will dry up lose its leaves and rot. The apple tree, however, is very much alive. It looks dead. It has no leaves, they will not grow until spring. It looks like a petrified collection of branches. But it is alive. In the spring it will sprout leaves, blossom and eventually bring a harvest of fruit.

You got it, it's the old 'don't be deceived by appearances' riddle, and as time goes on the true nature of each tree becomes evident. But who owns which tree? And which tree is represented by what family? The answer to the first question becomes somewhat obvious when viewed from a Christian viewpoint. Of course, the live tree belongs to God, while Satan takes possession of the dead tree. It is at this point, however, that the analogy begins to break down, unless we change it somewhat. The problem is that in real life there was in fact only one tree. The one and only tree was the dead one. Moreover, the tree did belong to God, until Satan came and stole it. Of course, the act of stealing it involved cutting it away from the root.

So we see the situation begin to unfold. God has a tree growing nicely. Satan comes along and cuts it off at the root and plants it without the root in the ground. God has a live root. Satan has a dead tree. Now the trouble has only just begun. And so our story begins...

In The Beginning

I marched through the large wooden doors into the spacious entrance hall of the Great Library. I turned to the right and climbed the wide stone staircase to the historical records department. This library contained the entire history of every living being in the whole of creation. Not only that, but there was a book detailing every thought and deed for each individual.

I always marvelled at how He had managed to do this, The Almighty One. He was always full of surprises and wonder but the level of detail contained in each book never ceased to amaze me. Since I was created to perform research, it should come as no great surprise that I enjoyed it so much. After all, the Creator never made anything or anyone without making them in such a way that they would be happiest and most fulfilled in doing what they had been created to do. Take people for instance, they were always striving and never truly fulfilled. All because most of them never got to grips with why they had been created. I suppose it's easier being an angel of my class. I mean, to be fair, I have never had to exercise any real faith. To be honest, I never quite understood humans anyway. All I had to do was gather the facts about an individual as required by the officials to the Great White Throne.

Usually finding the book I required was a long, time consuming process, but today was different. I was not working today. I was pursuing my special interest. Knowing that God had somehow put it in my heart to do this for a purpose was an interesting thought. What the purpose could be, I couldn't guess. He knows everything anyway.

I arrived at the librarian's reception desk. The duty librarian glowed brightly as I approached, his wings quivered giving the impression of great excitement. I stopped in front of the desk, but just before I could make my request, he spoke.

"I am pleased to see you, I have already found the books you require. The Almighty has already informed me of your needs."

"I have a desk and writer then?"

"Yes."

"And you have both books?"

"They are already at the table."

"Thank you."

I walked over to the desk, sat down and checked the books. They were indeed both there. Each book containing every thought and deed of the individuals concerned. The first was of The Word, the second The Morning Star. I opened them both. Being a research angel has advantages for this task. I can read many books and at the same time, write a summary. I am after all created to do just that. I had also brought the Bible with me as a reference point, and so I began...

Genesis 1:1 In the beginning God created the heavens and the earth.

So God created the heavens and the earth and everything in the universe. He created time and space. He created man to be a friend of God. He gave man dominion over all the earth. Man was given the choice to obey God and eat of the tree of life or to disobey and eat of the tree of knowledge. He was specifically warned that to eat of the tree of knowledge would mean he would have to die. Still man chose to disobey. Until then God had been able to walk with man and be his friend, now man had sinned and felt guilt. The relationship was broken. Although God was willing and able to forgive, man was incapable of receiving that forgiveness. He was, in effect, already dead to God.

And so was the beginning. I compared the accounts of The Word and The Morning Star with respect to these events.

The Word

Creating a universe is not easy. In Genesis, the Bible describes my Dad just speaking things into existence. Believe me, it is not that easy. It's simple, that's for sure, but not so easy.

The best way I can describe it is like putting together a jigsaw. A few thousand pieces all fit together to make a picture. Simple. A bit of patience and perseverance and it's done. Creating the universe is in principle that simple. But not as easy as it sounds. Imagine the universe as a jigsaw made of millions of pieces. What most people

don't realise, is that each piece is then itself a jigsaw. And each piece
of that a jigsaw itself. And then you have to know for each individual
piece of a piece of a piece which piece it is a part of. Add to all that,
the fact that we started with nothing and you may begin to understand.

You see, I am the Word. My Dad speaks and our Spirit moves so
that I become it. Hence the whole of creation came into existence
through me. It's so simple but not at all easy. Things are quite
straightforward. I mean they just have to be. But when it comes to
beings or personalities, it's not quite so easy. You see we have to
consider their desires and capabilities. We also have to take
responsibility for our creation.

At the end of the six days I was very pleased with what we had
done. It was good. And it would work just the way we wanted it to.
I knew before we started what it all meant. I knew what I would have
to do later. Even so, everything was okay.

The Morning Star

Part of my job is to protect The Word. It is perhaps the most
important job in heaven. I guess it makes me the most important
angel in heaven. I looked around. Heaven is a wonderful place and I
love the life I have. Looking at myself and everyone around me I can
see that my beauty surpasses them all. Actually, come to think of it, I
look better than the Creator does. In fact if I am to protect The Word
effectively, I guess I need to control it.

I pondered on these things as my servants came to me to collect
their instructions. I announced my plans. They were not surprised,
of course; they are intelligent beings and even an idiot could see that I
was right.

The next day we gathered before the Almighty. I thought carefully
how I would announce my intentions. Just as I gathered my thoughts
he spoke.

"Lucifer!"

"Yes," I replied.

"You have in mind to take charge of The Word?"

"Well, yes, I mean it makes sense doesn't it?"

"Explain yourself."

"I am the most beautiful thing in heaven. Every being knows that.
I am the cleverest, and wisest of all creation. It only makes sense that

I sit on the throne and rule. Such a perfect creation can be sustained and governed by me. I am able and willing."

"You are not able."

"I do not agree."

This was unexpected. The Creator had to agree. There was no reason why he shouldn't. I signalled to my servants and there was uproar. Angels began to take sides. They knew I was right. My beauty shone throughout heaven and many came to me. A few pathetic items went over to Him. Then without warning it began. A bright shining light burned under the throne. Angels poured out from it and began to fight with those on my side. We fought and fought. We were winning quite clearly when the light got so intense that it hurt. The pain began to grow until it wasn't worth sticking around. I called to my forces. We left heaven. No problem, I had my plans to get rid of heaven anyway.

I commanded my chief servants to gather and order our forces. As they departed I began to think. I realised I had a problem. That light was going to be difficult. I knew we could defeat it, but until we did, what could I do? The Creator could go anywhere with that light and I would have to leave. Heaven was effectively out of bounds. I could go back but it wasn't worth the hassle at this point. That only left one place to go: earth. I had no legal rights there though. The Creator could go there whenever he wanted. I needed a plan. I gathered the books of the law and studied. There had to be a way. Then I saw it. the Creator had given man dominion over all the earth. Now if I could get man to obey me and disobey Him then I would control that dominion. Not only that, but the Creator would suffer enormously because I knew how fond he was of Adam.

The Word

I love Adam. We made him in our image, but as yet he doesn't understand the full meaning of that. It's okay, he doesn't need to know yet. He knows good. He has everything he needs. I have given him the task of looking after the earth. It would be good if he had a companion to help though.

"Adam!"

"Yes, Lord?"

"How are you today?"

"Very happy, Lord, I have been naming the animals as you instructed."

"Well done. I would like to bless you with a partner, but you will need to trust me, okay?"

"Fine by me Lord, I know that you are good and that you love me beyond measure, I will trust you in anything."

"Very good, Adam. Remember it will be your responsibility to pass on all that I have told you to your new partner. If you will relax and sleep then I will make woman from out of you to be your companion."

"Okay, Lord, I will do everything you ask."

Adam fell asleep, and I made Eve from him. She was beautiful. The perfect mate for Adam. Adam woke and was also delighted. Afterwards I joined them each day and we talked together. It was good to be friends with Adam and Eve. We were all very happy. I knew that Lucifer was on the prowl, but I trusted Adam. Adam knew and did all that he was created to do. He looked after and loved his wife and they both had peace with me. Soon would be the time for them to eat of the tree of life so that they could live for ever with me. I looked forward to that moment.

The Morning Star

I knew a direct approach would fail with Adam. He was, after all, an intelligent being. The best approach would be to wrap the trap inside the truth. Deviously clever, I know. I would offer him the knowledge of good and evil, then he would be like Him. True they already knew good, and true they were already like Him. Furthermore, the only thing they had to gain was knowledge of evil, but so what? Dressed up like this, those suckers would fall for the ploy quite easily.

I entered the garden and waited by the tree. After a short while Adam and Eve came by. While Adam was distracted slightly, I spoke to Eve.

"Eve!"

"Oh, hello, my you are very beautiful!"

"Yes, and I have a suggestion."

"What is it?"

"Are you aware of the fact that if you eat of the tree of knowledge, you will know both good and evil, and you will be just like God?"

"Really? No, I am sure we will die if we do."

"Of course you won't, God wouldn't want to deny you such knowledge, besides how can you die if you're like him. Can he die?"

Eve was not entirely convinced. So while she tried to remember the Creator's instructions through Adam, I sent Doubt to molest her thoughts. Doubt did a great job (under my instruction) and my timing was perfect. She reached for the fruit and ate, this was too easy. Adam saw it all, but I managed to stop him interfering by sending Complacency and Sloth. Those two together can stop anybody achieving anything. Now when Adam saw that Eve didn't drop dead, it became a pushover, Envy and Lust just helped fill his head with some useful ideas and he ate too. Bingo! A real coup. Now we all backed off and I sat thinking.

So far so good. I now had the legal right to rule Man, and through him the earth. The entire earth was my dominion. And the Creator would have to put up with it, and cry over his poor little Adam. Then the idea came to me. The Creator had said that if Adam ate of the tree of knowledge then he would die. If I could get Adam to eat of the tree of life, he would live for ever and so the Creator would be proved wrong. That would give me the legal right to enter and rule in heaven. Excellent. This was just so easy. First I would need to inform my high council.

The council had gathered. I had explained my plan. Death was not impressed. He was quite adamant in fact.

"I demand the right to take them both now," Death shrieked.

"Calm down," I gently persuaded. "Just think, you can have more than just two if you wait."

"But if they eat of the tree of life then I lose my right to take them."

"We will wait until they have children, then we will ensure that Sickness destroys their ability to reproduce. Then they can eat of the tree of life and live for ever. That will prove Him wrong. You will be able to take any and all of his descendants provided they do not personally eat of the tree of life, and we can ensure that they don't."

"But I want them now."

"You will obey me, and me only!"

He saw reason. Two now or countless millions in future. He knew I was right. And so the council agreed. The plan could not fail. My first plan worked, it even opened up the opportunity of getting back into heaven legally and getting rid of that Light. I smiled to myself, I really am quite clever.

The Word

Later that day, I began my usual walk to meet Adam. Of course, he was not at the usual spot. I knew what had happened and my heart was heavy with grief. I was also feeling very angry. However, I had known all along what was to happen and so I pushed my raging emotions to one side and proceeded to deal with the situation. It really did look quite bleak. Adam and Eve had disobeyed me.

The problem was not forgiving them, I was willing to do that as much as my Dad was. The problem was dealing with the consequences of their action. To start with, my Spirit which I had breathed into them, with which I had given them life, had left them. My Spirit cannot be where sin is and so at the moment of disobedience my Spirit which gave them life departed from them. They were now just flesh. They were dead. As surely as a block of stone has no life in it, so Adam and Eve were devoid of life. Dead sticks instead of live trees. Worse than that was the fact that although the real essence of life had gone, and so given Death the power to enter and consume them, they themselves would still think that they had life.

There was another issue: The tree of life. Dad had so designed the flesh that if it ate of the tree of life, it would live for ever. Now if Adam or Eve ate of the tree of life, their flesh would live for ever, and yet they were really dead. Can you imagine it? An eternal living death. Add to this that Lucifer would have power over them as long as their flesh lived. So Lucifer now had the legal right to reign over the flesh of Adam and Eve, and through them over all the earth.

Lastly and perhaps most distressing, was that all their descendants would be the same. I had no legal way at this point of getting my Spirit within them. The entire human race was doomed to be in this state of sin and separation from my Spirit. They would fear rather than love me.

My Father, the Spirit and I had gathered and discussed this situation even before creation. It was not that I did not know what to do, it was just that I knew that what I was about to do would seem very harsh to Adam. He would not understand at this point that it was for his own good.

I threw them both out of the garden and sealed it so that they could not get back and eat of the tree of life. They now knew evil as well as the good they had once known and it would manifest itself in their dead lives and experience. The man, who was created to tend and have dominion over the earth would now find that the earth rebelled against him and forced him to work hard to survive, even for the few years that his flesh would live. The woman, who was to joyously and happily bear children, would now suffer pain in birth. Finally I made them a promise. I promised that one of their descendants would trample Lucifer under his feet. Lucifer would have the power to strike back at his heel as his head was crushed under it.

It had begun. There was much work to do. To bring about my promise would involve a lot of risks. I knew that Lucifer would use his new found position of power to his best advantage. There could be no mercy for him. He had set himself against my Father and so against me and my Spirit. He would try and set himself up as our equal, and he would try and inflict as much pain as possible. To him, humanity was just a tool to be used to that end. And so it began...

The Morning Star

I stormed into the council chamber. I was not pleased. I glared at those present. Each and every one of them sat silently watching my every move. Fear gloated over everyone. Anger paraded himself around the table. I sat down and searched for the one responsible.

"Legalism, where are you?" I demanded.

"Just here, Your Majesty." Legalism leant forward and revealed himself, until then hidden behind Pride. Legalism and Pride often worked together. I knew that to confront Legalism here in front of everybody would be a waste of time. I would need to gather facts first. He would never admit to any fault. He of all of us knew and studied every word of Him.

"Why was I not informed that the way to the tree of life could be barred?" I inquired.

"No one knew, Your Majesty," Legalism knowingly responded.

"But it is your job to know the Law and what is possible."

"Your Majesty, as yet we have very few words to study. It is only realistic at this point to define what is not allowed. I am a legalist, as such I can tell you what is not allowed, what must be done, and legal consequences of actions. I cannot be expected to think of new things to do, or to list every possible allowable action. Such a lofty achievement is only possible with your insight, wisdom and methods."

"What you say is, of course, true." I knew he would try this approach, I had to save face quickly.

"I had anticipated these latest moves on the Creator's part, but I wanted to see how sharp each of you were. I had hoped that at least one of you might have proved worthy of being chairman of this council. As it is, I am the only one able to perform the task. Unfortunately for you all, I shall be busy for the foreseeable future (which in my case is a long time). I therefore disband this council and decree that you will all report to me individually from now on. We will be able to operate far more efficiently if you each concentrate on your own tasks rather than spend so much time concerned with others. As and when some of you need to work together it will be under my personal direction. If anyone disagrees with me, let him speak now."

You could have heard a pin drop. Not a sound. There was no way that these inferior creatures could argue with me. All I had to do now was wait. Flattery would speak soon. He would not be able to resist this opportunity to show off in front of them all...

"Your Majesty," Flattery chimed, "such wisdom and understanding as yours is unequalled among us. I am sure that I speak for us all when I say that such an excellent and perfect way as yours must be followed. You are indeed magnificent!"

"Very well then," I conceded, "we will operate in the manner we have agreed. Legalism, stay here, the rest of you are dismissed."

Silently they filed out. After what seemed like hours, Legalism and I were left alone. We sat in silence for some time. Legalism was clearly pleased with himself. I was not so happy. I was bothered by this promise of the Creator's. Finally I began.

"Well what do you make of it?" I inquired.

"The promise you mean?" he asked.

"Of course."

"Well, on the face of it, it's not a problem. The Creator has promised that one of their offspring will, how should I put this, crush Your Majesty. However, since you have authority over the entire human race, I fail to see how he can achieve it."

"Are you sure there are no loopholes? I mean, I do have dominion over every being that can or will be born of man."

"Absolutely, Your Majesty. From a legal point of view, it is technically impossible for any human to have authority over you."

"Is there a way the Creator can enter the earth legally?"

"Your Majesty, please relax. Man was given dominion over the earth. You now have dominion over Man. Under the law you have absolute authority throughout the earth."

"But the Creator owns the earth?"

"Yes, but he has delegated his authority to man and you have dominion over man. It is truly all yours."

"So how can he fulfil this promise?"

"I see no way legally that he can."

"This is interesting. Tell me, what are the consequences if the Creator fails to fulfil his promise?"

"Your Majesty, if the Creator fails to fulfil any promise, or if he breaks any of his laws, then The Word fails. Failure of any single part means that the whole fails. If this happens, his throne collapses, heaven itself falls, and the Creator is reduced to a liar. You have dominion over Lies and as such you would have dominion over Him."

"Indeed, so you are saying that all I have to do is prove one word of his wrong and the entire universe becomes mine?"

"In a nutshell, Your Majesty, yes."

"Then I have much to plan. I shall no doubt require you again, so do not go far. However, I want you to study continuously every letter of every word the Creator speaks. Remember, if you find the slightest fault in the law then it is through you that I shall accomplish this, and you will be rewarded. Now leave."

"As you wish."

Legalism hurried away. This was indeed exciting news. So all I have to do is get Him into a legal corner. This was going to be a breeze. I was bothered about the confidence the Creator seemed to have. Never mind; it was irrelevant, the Creator had already made a mistake. After all, how could he crush me here on earth with a human being when I had dominion over both. I really am so clever...

Noah, The Flood and Babel

I took a short break. I leant back and thought to myself, I was in fact very surprised. Lucifer, or Satan as we called him, was quite a remarkable character. Just from reading as far as this, and knowing the truth, it was clear to me that he was as successful at deceiving himself as others. I mean he really did believe that he could outsmart God.

I looked around. I was alone at my desk. I was pleased to be in heaven, in eternity. No matter how quickly or slowly I did this work, it mattered not. In eternity everything is to come, everything is happening, and everything has happened. I was outside time. I could work at my own pace, and know that I would be finished when the results were needed. Heaven, what a wonderful place.

From a historical point of view I was now to consider the events and pressures surrounding Noah and the flood. Fairly quickly afterwards came the building of a tower at the city of Babel. It was during these two events that God and Satan effectively marked out their respective strategies and manners of working. Interestingly, it seems at this point that God is fighting a rear guard action. It appears to all intents and purposes that He has lost control of the earth and can only limit Satan's activities by direct and catastrophic intervention. Such interventions always give the impression of being bad news for man.

Noah was the best of a very bad lot. God found in him a willingness to hear his voice and obey it. That was crucial. So while God quite righteously wanted to destroy humanity and start again, there was one man through whom God could begin his work of salvation. So God made a flood and of course provided Noah with the instructions to build a boat and save pairs of every kind of living creature. The flood came, Noah and his family were saved. God established a covenant with Noah never to try and destroy mankind again.

However, a few generations later mankind was almost as bad as before. Their arrogance and pride made them think that they could get to heaven themselves. The manifestation of this kind of thinking was the Tower of Babel which was meant to reach to heaven. So God had to intervene and put an end to their exploits. Scattering mankind over the surface of the earth and confusing their language achieved the objective, bringing their vain imaginations to nought.

The Word

Dad and I discussed and agreed our plan with the Holy Spirit. It was going to be tough. At some point I would have to go to earth as a human. Just the thought made me shiver. I must not concern myself with that now, however, as I still had plenty to do.

In order to save mankind I had a number of things to do. I would have to establish a new way for man to relate to my Dad. The only way this is possible when not in his 'presence' is through the Holy Spirit. Unfortunately in his present state of 'deadness' he is incapable of receiving the Spirit. There are exceptions, of course, such as Enoch. But these exceptions are just the Spirit bringing back to life man's dead spirit.

The first step was to demonstrate to man the principles of my Dad's righteous judgement, a covenant, and my Dad's grace. The judgement was to be the destruction of every living thing on earth. This would allow a new start. The covenant would be based on a man trusting God, and not his own knowledge, for salvation from the judgement. The grace would be the position (by revelation) of the information required, the safe passage through the judgement and finally a promise and sign for the man and his family to remember it by.

I looked through early history to find such a man. There was a suitable candidate. He was as good as he could be. Looking into his heart I saw a man who wanted to serve my Father. I could find no others on earth at that time. They were all evil, and intent on more evil.

I studied Noah carefully. Not perfect but willing. I revealed my plans to him. I gave him precise instructions on what to do. He faithfully did as I said. I knew the Holy Spirit was working in this man. There was no way he could have managed otherwise, especially with the peer pressure to which he was subjected. It just about ruined the plan actually. How would you feel building a boat in the middle of Iran? Your friends ask you why and you have to explain that it is going to rain so much that you will be able to have a holiday in it. Then you start gathering animals of every kind, while your friends are out at parties. If Lucifer had ever understood what was really going on he would have stopped it for sure. Well, he had chosen darkness and lies and so let him live it. Noah had done a good job. He entered the ark. Now someone had to shut the door and this was tricky. Not from a technical point of view you realise, but from a legal standpoint. It rather relied on Noah letting me do it. You see, he had the instructions but the whole thing fell apart when it came to the door. If he didn't exercise faith and believe my instructions then I wouldn't be allowed to close the door. Good old Noah; he did, I closed the door and we were set.

Timing is crucial with all this stuff. You remember the analogy of the jigsaw in creation? Well here comes the punch line: I had to create the earth in such a way that there was enough cloud cover to make a one-off flood of the entire land surface of the planet. Furthermore, the climate had to be unstable enough to cause the flood, while being stable enough for it to be delayed until this very moment. I have to admit to a little smile of self satisfaction when it worked so well. That's what I meant in Genesis when I said 'It was good'. That is my smile of 'got it right'. I digress. The rains came, the floods rose and judgement was complete. The floods receded. The climate of the planet was irreversibly changed. Once entirely covered in cloud, the surface of the earth was for the first time exposed to the sun's rays. A rainbow appeared. For the physicists among you, you will know that you can only get a rainbow with direct sunlight. The direct sunlight was only available because the cloud covering which caused the flood had gone. It would not be possible to repeat this particular incident, because never again would enough clouds gather over the whole planet. The rainbow therefore served as a useful sign that there would never be another flood like it. I love it when a plan comes together.

The Morning Star

I brooded silently. I didn't enjoy not knowing why the Creator had done something. Why had he destroyed everyone, but saved one man? I hadn't lost any authority over him. True, it annoyed me that he could command Death to take people without my permission. But then I could command Death to take people too. No problem. These humans were better to me alive anyway, with certain exceptions, of course. Still the reason was not clear. If the Creator wanted to destroy humanity he was allowed to, but why not complete the job? Why do it but then spare one man? It just didn't make sense.

I scowled to myself. It was time to gather more facts. I sent out for reports from the minions. As each spirit came in, they gave their reports and left. Only one of them gave me a lead.

"Your Highness, I have found that there is something significant about this man," chirped Doubt merrily.

"And what is that, you loathsome creature?" I inquired.

"Only this Noah, of all the humans at that time, had any resistance to me."

"Explain yourself."

"All the other humans readily accepted thoughts and thinking that doubted the existence of the Creator. It was easy to make them believe that he probably didn't exist and if he did, then he didn't care. However, Noah was different. He was firm in his belief that the Creator existed. Not just that, but he seemed to possess faith enough to hear and obey the Creator's voice!"

"But you told me that no one with such faith existed. You informed me that you had everyone doubting sufficiently to render them unreachable by the Creator." I checked myself, I had to be careful not to give away any sign of confusion or lack of knowledge, "I had of course anticipated this whole episode. You, however, have not performed to my satisfaction. Giving me misleading reports concerning these humans could have been very costly, had it not been for my foresight."

"But Your Highness..."

"Silence! You are to continue planting seeds in every human. They must not be allowed to reach this level of awareness again. Do you understand me?"

"Yes, Your Highness."

"You are excused."

Doubt abruptly left. Clearly there was something here that I needed to check. This was the Creator's doing. He was responsible for the faith in this 'Noah'. I needed to consult Legalism. Perhaps, the Creator had illegally entered earth. Legalism came with his factual report on the events. It made interesting reading. There were two essential details that I just knew must be illegal. I pointed these out to Legalism.

"So the Creator spoke with this man Noah," I announced.

"Indeed, Your Highness," Legalism replied.

"And then proceeded to close the door to the ark."

"That is correct."

"Now, concerning the first, is this legal?"

"I see no reason why not, Your Highness, there is nothing legally to stop the Creator talking to anyone, the only question is, do they really believe it is him?"

"You mean the Creator can just stroll up to any human at any time and talk to them?"

"Yes, Your Highness."

"Then why hasn't he been doing it ever since Adam?"

"It is a little more complex than that, Your Highness, you understand that the Creator cannot reveal himself fully in front of a human."

"Of course I know that, you fool, these pathetic humans would be immediately consumed by his light."

"Well, he must therefore communicate through an intermediary, and that takes faith on the part of the hearer. Until this 'Noah' turned up we had managed to create enough doubt in the humans that it was impossible for them to believe it could be the Creator speaking."

"I see," this was beginning to go round in circles. "But what of this act of the Creator's in closing the ark?"

"All perfectly legal, Your Highness; it worked like this. The Creator speaks to Noah, and Noah responds from earth by building the ark and entering it. This gives the Creator the right to respond to Noah. Legally all the Creator did was respond to Noah's response to himself. That is legal."

"You mean the Creator can respond to acts of faith by humans?"

"Provided that act of faith is in itself a response to the Creator."

"Well, what can be done to stop this?"

"Nothing, Your Highness, except of course to prevent these humans acting in faith. And that should be easy, because we can monitor whenever any contact is made by the Creator and then take countermeasures to prevent the act of faith."

This was turning out to be okay after all. If the Creator was limited to such activities then he really was at my mercy. It would be simple to frustrate his attempts to regain control of the earth.

I sat back and brooded more. A three pronged attack was essential. One to limit and hold any of the Creator's activities on the earth. Number two would continually challenge His Word and make him seem a liar. The third would be to set up and confirm my own dominions in the earth, with enough power and glory to beat heaven. If any one of these approaches succeeded then I would win. The Creator would fall and I would be able to ascend to my rightful place at the throne of heaven.

By the time a couple of generations had passed, Noah would be forgotten. His descendants were only too eager to follow my superior ways. I had my spirits effectively organised, each one with a hierarchy of spirits below him to manage and control this human race. In this way, limiting the Creator's activities became easy. In fact, he hadn't even been around to see what was going on for years. So far, my legal experts had failed to come up with a failing in His Word but it was just a matter of time, and I had plenty of that. However, my best success had been in establishing my power on earth. Because of my excellent planning, the whole of mankind was all too eager to collaborate and help me make my way into heaven. They had even become infected with my ideas themselves. My latest brainchild was to build a tower to hold all this knowledge and glory. In spirit it would reach the heavens and allow me righteous and legal re-entry into heaven. The whole of mankind serving my every purpose would indeed make me better than the Creator.

The Word

It had now been some time since I had been to earth. However, that did not mean that I did not know what was going on. Indeed I was only too well aware of the depraved leanings of mankind. Men would do what men would do. Urged on by original desire and lust to be like God, a desire placed and fed by Satan himself, men were now attempting to reach the heavens with their achievements. All of them, however, were dead works. Little did they realise that although they could achieve anything, eternal life was impossible without my Spirit. The Holy Spirit was not something they could get, it could only be given by my Dad.

I announced the problem, "If humans acting as one person can do this, then nothing they can imagine will be impossible."

The time had come to humble them slightly. Just enough to let them realise that all their striving, all their achievements would be in vain unless they were motivated by my Spirit. It was true that they could and would, through knowledge achieve anything they wanted, but what good would achievement do them if they remained in a state of sin? It would not be possible for them to gain peace, hope and all the other fruits of my Spirit without my Spirit.

So as one, Dad, The Holy Spirit and myself went to earth. First, we scattered each family or clan to a different part of the earth. The first natural consequence of this was that each group evolved their own ways of expressing themselves, they changed the way they spoke. Within a very short time, each group was speaking differently, in different languages. Split up in such a way, the project of building the Tower of Babel was impossible, and came to a halt.

The Morning Star

"Interfering like this is outrageous!" I screamed at everyone present, "He has no right."

"Unfortunately, Your Highness, the Creator does indeed have the legal basis for such action," Legalism ventured somewhat sheepishly.

"On what grounds?" I demanded, reasserting my normal, perfect poise.

"He is allowed, at this point, to act as judge and so pass judgements as he sees fit. Naturally if we can demonstrate that such a judgement is unjust then we have him."

"Yes, I know that!" I snapped. I sat and thought. Legalism and Fear fidgeted, while Pride and Arrogance looked pan-faced at me. "But The Word said something very interesting, something about being able to do anything they desire, now doesn't that allow us all the leeway we desire ?"

"Indeed," cooed Pride, as Arrogance nodded, "If we can get these humans acting as one then The Word has defined that they will achieve anything they can imagine."

"But to make them act as one means that they must trust each other," complained Fear, "and I simply cannot allow anything but Mistrust to grow."

"Fools!" I overruled. "There is more than one way to deal with this. We can use Fear to help us steer them all in the same direction. My direction. By definition they will then be acting as one. This Creator has again stumbled and made our task easier."

"You are, of course, correct in your analysis, Your Highness!" ventured Legalism, desperate to please me.

"Excellent!" I finished, "Send Witchcraft in as you leave."

Witchcraft entered with a sneer at the others as they left. He bowed and acknowledged my greatness before asking permission to sit. I granted his request and we began.

"You have some task for me, Your Perfection," Witchcraft ventured.

"Yes," I replied. "This should be perfect for your devious ways. I want you to start possessing as many of these humans as you can. Do your usual, of promising them they will get their way, or promise them that it's for the greater good if you wish, but I want you to get as many as possible."

"Of course."

"Furthermore, you will need to be clever in your approach to the other spirits. Invariably they will allow you easier access if you agree to allow them access to humans whom they have not yet managed to hold."

"I know I can manage that."

"I need you to report directly to me. Try and be subtle wherever possible but if that doesn't work then feel free to dominate and intimidate."

"A pleasure, Your Highness."

"Yes, and one final thing, if you perceive your powers being curtailed in any way, I need to know."

"I am sure that will not happen."

"I am sure it will, the Creator will not allow you free reign for long, I am certain. It is therefore imperative that I know if, and when you meet any resistance!"

"As you wish, Wise One."

"Enough, you are dismissed. On your way out send in Pagan."

Witchcraft turned and left. He would be busy. His many minions would be even busier. I was pleased. Pagan entered. I am not sure that Pagan is the best name for him really. Perhaps Chameleon would be better. He could appear as just about any god that any human wanted to worship. Sun, stars, weather, war, fertility, whatever. It was all him. Of course, in worshipping him they were really worshipping me, and very soon I would be able to sweep him aside so that these wretched humans could worship me directly. Some of them already did anyway.

Pagan did look good. He was one of the few spirits that I allowed to look almost as good as me. It was dangerous, since he would not be happy to let me receive worship, however, that was my right.

"So in view of the scattering, what do you intend?" I asked.

"There is no problem, Glorious One, in fact the task becomes easier. The different cultures and languages that are developing allow me to present many different faces and be accepted. If one face does not work then it becomes easy to entrap these humans with another."

"Good. I want every one of these vile humans worshipping you in one form or another. I don't care how you do it. Promise them anything you like. Just make the lies appear believable."

"As you wish," Pagan gloated.

Pagan was delighted, as was Witchcraft. With so many spirits using such diverse angles of approach it was easy to take these humans. Just a little more time and they would all be in my hands. Then I could go to heaven and challenge the Creator. Why did I have to wait though? It was already obvious that I was going to win. This charade was beginning to irritate me. It was after all just a matter of time.

Abraham

At this point in history God chose to establish yet another covenant. It took the whole of a man's life to do, but he got there. Satan in the meantime busied himself creating counterfeits and blockages to God's will. Things seemed all but lost for God after the last episode, but he had plans. First Abraham was promised a son who would be heir to God's promise. Satan managed to fool Abraham into accepting second best, a son by his servant girl. In due course, however, God's promise held true. Then came the affair of God asking Abraham to give him Isaac. Abraham complied, but God intervened again to provide the required sacrifice. The deed was recorded as if done as requested. Isaac later fathered Jacob and Esau. Esau, the elder brother, sold his birthright to Jacob and so lost the promise of God's covenant. Jacob, although selected by God to receive the promise, still resorted to dishonest means to 'steal' the blessing from his father. And so Jacob (then called Israel, which means to struggle with God) lived with his Uncle Laban for a while, only to find that Laban was a bigger cheat than he was. Over time Jacob had many children. This family was destined to become the nation of Israel, a people set aside for God. The spiritual battle, however, was only just warming up.

The Word

Of all the people on earth, I finally found one with faith. Faith is like trust and risk mixed together: the trust part is believing in something or someone; the risk part is acting as if what you believe is true. The best example is a bank account. If the statement comes through and tells you that you have £100 in the account then you tend to believe it. You then act by signing a cheque or a debit instruction when you buy something. That is faith at work. You believe that you have something and you act as though you have. Of course, in this case, the faith is created by a written statement from the bank.

Similarly, faith works in my Kingdom. I can say something, you can believe it and act on it – faith. But if I say something and you don't believe it, or you believe it but don't act, then that is lack of faith or doubt. Of course, the facts are facts whether or not you believe them. Like the bank account, you may have £100 but if you don't have the faith to use it, then it appears as if you don't have it.

And so it was at this time. Most people didn't even believe. Some did but would not act. Useless. To them I didn't exist. But of course I do exist. That is a fact, and no lack of faith can change the fact, only the perception of it. Abraham was a man with faith. He had a lot, and he was going to need it.

Abraham (or Abram as he was called originally) lived in Ur. The place was a cauldron of man's ways of thinking. I wanted to build Abraham's faith and to do so I needed him to start exercising it. I told him to leave Ur. I told him that although he and his wife were too old to have children, I would make him a father of many nations. He believed. He had faith. He acted. He left Ur. This was excellent.

I promised him and his descendants the land of Canaan. He believed me. He trusted me. Now we were going places.

The Morning Star

Doubt crept in to see me. He looked like Death. Very unhappy. I could guess why.

Someone with faith had turned up again. This would have to be handled with skill.

"Yes, what is it, have you lost control of someone?" I pre-empted.

"Your Highness, my power is limited, I could not hold him..." Doubt fumbled for the right way to let me know.

"I am aware of your predicament, who is this human?"

"Abram."

"I see. And he has acted as well as believed?"

"Yes, Your Highness, he left Ur and so the task of influencing him became that much harder."

"And the promise he was given?"

"That he would be the father of many nations, Your Highness."

"Interesting, but I see that he is old; to receive such a promise will take far more faith than he has now."

"Yes, Your Highness, but his act of obedience in leaving Ur allows his faith to grow daily, it will not be long."

"Then we must act, I will provide you with special support from Fear and Witchcraft. Send in Fear as you leave." I dismissed him.

Such an event was to be predicted. The Creator was clearly attempting to gain legal entry to earth through faith, but this could be stopped. It would need Fear to undermine his faith and so allow Doubt to creep in again. As an added measure, a bit of Witchcraft would help thwart any designs of the Creator. Fear entered into my presence.

"Your Highness," he bowed.

"Go and attack Abraham, personally!" I demanded. "You must get him to lie. He has gone to Egypt. If you can get him to deny his wife, then we can cause him trouble in Egypt. This will lower his resistance to Doubt. I want you to ensure that Doubt gets a foothold ready for Witchcraft to make his move."

"As you command, Your Highness," Fear left and Witchcraft entered.

"I have a special task for you," I informed Witchcraft.

"Delighted, Most Wise One," he replied.

"Follow Fear and Doubt and as soon as the opportunity avails itself, persuade Abram to have a child by his servant girl."

"I see. But why?"

"That is my business, you must just obey."

"As you say, Your Excellence." He bowed and left.

The plan worked. Of course it worked. Abraham had a son, Ishmael, by his servant girl.

He was the firstborn of Abraham. Excellent. Now I just had to sit back and wait for the Creator's promise to fail or to tie itself up in knots.

The Word

A setback. In fact it was a mess. Now I not only had to deliver the promise but I would also have to establish the precedence of the firstborn not necessarily being God's choice. This was going to cause big problems, especially in the distant future. Well, I would just have to use these problems for the good of my people.

I sent messengers to Abraham to confirm my promise. Doubt was there, but Abraham's faith held and a son was born to his wife. Isaac, the fruit of my promise to Abraham. Now for the real test.

I called Abraham to give his son Isaac to me. I had promised that he would be the father of many nations. This instruction would seem contradictory. Abraham was full of pain at the thought but took his son and readied to sacrifice him. How Abraham must have felt when his son asked where the sacrifice was! Yet he responded perfectly and spoke words of mighty faith that shook the heavens. He said that I would provide. This gave me the legal right to do just that. At the last moment, I provided a ram for him to kill instead of his son. The key to this whole episode was that he had indeed offered his son to me.

The legal precedent was now set. Not only had Abraham in faith accepted and stated that I would provide, but he had offered his son. The stage was set for me to be sent to earth and offered in return. The legality was established by his offer, since my Dad could now argue that he owed me (his son) to Abraham and hence all his descendants.

First there was a nation to build, and the small matter of my Dad's sovereign right to choose to establish. Then there would be many more tasks to complete before it was the right time for me to go down to earth. But today there had been progress. The other legal precedent that was established, was that Abraham's descendants (through Isaac) belonged to me. They would be my people.

The Morning Star

Legalism approached as I sat unhappily considering the possibility of failure. I already knew that he approached with bad news. I had heard heaven rejoicing. Just the noise was enough to put me in a bad mood but it clearly meant more than that. Something very bad had happened, and I was going to make someone pay.

"I have news, Your Highness." Legalism spoke softly hoping not to disturb me.

"Bad news?" I grunted.

"Very grave, Your Highness."

"Very well, we will discuss this matter now."

"As you wish."

"Well, what is it?"

"The Creator has managed to get a legal foothold on the earth!"

"What!" This was worse than I'd imagined, but I composed myself and gave the impression that I had anticipated it.

"Yes, this Abraham offered the Creator his son."

"But it was not accepted!" I knew more than he thought.

"The offer was sufficient to allow the Creator to do the same for Abraham or any of his descendants."

"Such a move was expected." I composed myself.

"Sorry?" Legalism seemed puzzled by this.

"Yes," I pressed my advantage. "This means that at some point we will have the opportunity to trap this Son of his, The Word."

"A most delightful prospect, Your Highness."

"Indeed," I smiled to myself, actually I had said nothing untrue so I was probably right.

"There is one further thing, Your Highness."

"Yes?"

"The matter of his descendants, the Creator will be able to claim them for his own!"

"And no doubt he will claim that heaven and earth belong to him, but they are still captive to sin, and so to me," I gloated.

"But he will be able to teach them his ways."

"No matter," I explained. "All that will do is highlight how short they fall of his way. That provides an excellent opportunity for Guilt to invade their stupid minds and break down the relationship further."

"I see," said Legalism.

"Yes, I want you to keep a close eye on all further revelations and assist Guilt in this task."

"Excellent, Your Majesty."

"Now leave me, I need to think."

Legalism departed, clearly helped by my wisdom and insight into the situation. Indeed my approach need not change. The fact that the Creator would be able to operate a little more freely on earth now would prove to be my advantage. A little like laying a trap and waiting for someone to enter. So let The Word think that progress had been made. Operating on earth through men of faith would be his downfall. Sinful men could be relied on to let him down. Then I would pounce.

The Word

Isaac had two sons, Esau the firstborn and Jacob the second. Esau was a man with no real faith. He preferred to rely on his own skill and expertise as a hunter to make his way. Jacob, although a bit of a mother's boy, did have potential. He was a cheat, it was true. But he was aware of his own weakness. He could be taught to rely on me. He would struggle for sure.

Here was also the most excellent opportunity to demonstrate on earth that my father's sovereign will and choice prevails. Esau was the firstborn, the heir to the father, and therefore legally entitled to receive my promise to Abraham and Isaac.

Esau was, it is true, his father's favourite. However, he was not my Dad's choice. Day after day he would come home and impress his father with the animals he had hunted. One particular day though, he failed to catch anything. He spent so long away from home that by the time he returned he was very hungry. Jacob, having been at home all the time, saw his opportunity and offered him a meal, but at a price. The price was Esau's birthright. Now Esau, who did not consider my promise (just shows how little he valued and thought about it), accepted. And so the legality of what was to follow was established. Esau forgot all about the incident but Jacob never did.

Years later, Isaac sent for Esau and asked him to catch him a nice meal. He would then give Esau his blessing. Jacob placed great value on the blessing and now considered it his. His heart was still full of trickery and deceit, and he did not yet trust me. So he schemed and pretended to be Esau, full of lies and hypocrisy he received the blessing from Isaac. Once Esau returned and Isaac discovered the truth Esau began to hate Jacob. Isaac could not withdraw the blessing he gave to Jacob. Jacob therefore received the blessing of both Esau and Jacob. My Dad's sovereign choice was established legally.

The Morning Star

This was excellent. I studied the events as they unfolded and was delighted. The Creator had allowed this Jacob, a liar and a cheat, to receive his promise – he had even cheated to get it! With this kind of precedent to work with, it was going to be easy to be in control of that blessing. It was a shame, of course, that Esau had not inherited the promise. A man with so much trust in his own strength is so much easier to control. Jacob did provide a small problem as he had exercised enough faith to consider the blessing worth having, Esau had not. Cheating and conniving were methods of which I fully approved, in this case. It left Jacob wide open for me to try and cheat him of the blessing. The Creator would have to let me gently cheat the promise out of his hands.

Jacob went to stay with his Uncle Laban. Laban was wonderful; he was a bigger cheat than Jacob. Jacob fell for Laban's youngest daughter and agreed to work for seven years in order to have her as his wife. What an opportunity! Having spent seven years of his life working for Laban, Jacob received not the daughter he wanted but the elder one, and he certainly didn't rate her. He had been tricked and had to agree to another seven years to get the wife he wanted. This was like taking candy from a baby. Now I had the ideal set-up to get Jacob to have a family so divided by jealousy that it would be easy to rob him of his blessings.

Then there was a small incident I felt increasingly unhappy about. Jacob left Laban and began to return to the Land of Canaan. Laban was not happy and pursued him. After a bit of a showdown, Laban left in peace and Jacob continued onward. Jacob, conniving as ever, prepared gifts for his brother Esau in order to buy peace; he still feared that Esau would have it in his mind to kill him. That night, an angel wrestled with Jacob. Not that I am worried about the angel but he seemed to let Jacob win. Furthermore he allowed Jacob to extract a further blessing from him. Finally, he changed Jacob's name to Israel. This was what I didn't like. When the Creator changes peoples names it is significant. I knew that from Abraham. Abraham was Abram and the Creator changed his name to Abraham which means 'father of many nations'. Now he had changed Jacob (which means 'deceiver', and was rather appropriate) to Israel (which means 'to struggle with God'). I somehow felt that I had lost something. Yet to have this lineage of blessing from the Creator, so named that it would struggle against him, seemed to play into my hands. I was uneasy.

I pondered. This 'Israel' was significant. The Creator had it clearly in his mind to try and bring his precious promises to pass through Israel. I therefore had to oppose him. I had to try and lead him and his descendants in my ways and away from the Creator's ways. It would also be useful to use the other people of the world to resist him. In fact, if I could destroy Israel then the Creator would be unable to fulfil his promise and my purpose would be achieved. The critical point. All I had to do was prove that the Creator had lied or that The Word had failed and I would win.

I called some of my higher minions to a meeting in order to explain our new approach. What was now needed was a planned approach to achieve my objective. The many pathetic creatures filed in and stood before me.

"I know that I said such meetings would not be required," I announced, "however, special circumstances have come about, in accordance with my planning, that require a full appraisal of the current situation. Our activities will be shifted somewhat in emphasis, since the Creator has now allowed a more specific target to develop. Legalism, your report!"

"Your Highness," Legalism began, "the Creator has established that his promises will come to pass through Israel."

There were cackles of delight around the room. Some of these demons began discussing the matter among themselves. None listening, all of them competing for the legal right to first hold over some part of Israel and his children.

"Silence!" I commanded. "No one shall speak until I invite him. Let us continue, Legalism."

"This provides us with some interesting opportunities," Legalism went on, "to start with, it would appear that the Creator has all but abandoned the rest of humanity to us. In addition, the position with Israel is better for us than it was with Noah after the flood."

"Indeed," I ventured, "but what of this legal right that the Creator appears to have, to call any one of you to do his bidding."

"Well, well," Legalism shifted uncomfortably. "I was in court just the other day to establish this matter. It seems that the Creator can indeed command us to perform specific tasks within our power, without your agreement, Your Highness."

"That does not matter," I reassured the faces in the room, which had suddenly began to show signs of extreme concern, "since you can only do what is in your power, and hence within your characters, any command you are required to perform can only benefit our cause." This seemed to put a few minds at rest. Indeed so it should. Such an elementary conclusion was obvious. I went on, "Just see to it that I am informed of any such command by the Creator, so that we can take full advantage of its effects." I slowed towards the end of my sentence, allowing the full impact to soak in.

"The most lucrative and beneficial course of action is obvious," announced Legalism. "We must destroy Israel, or make the Creator so angry with him that he destroys Israel. Given our successes so far, this should not prove difficult for the rest of you. I will, of course, be available to assist you all in this endeavour."

"Excellent!" I gloated. "And now Pagan, I believe you have some good news for us?"

"Yes indeed," Pagan enthused. "Rachel, Israel's favourite wife, has kept all the manifestations of me from her father Laban's house. This provides us all with an excellent opportunity to continue infiltrating and influencing the entire family."

"Good, and there are more..." I invited each in turn.

"I have petty hurts and favouritism running through the whole family," added Jealousy, "Joseph even has a special coat now, and his brothers are on the verge of killing him in rage!"

"We are now so much a part of their lives," chorused Deceit and Witchcraft, "that they don't even know it's us at work. They think it's all just natural."

"I am finding it easy to penetrate the thoughts of the children," volunteered Doubt, "thanks to the father and his favouritism, they have no faith left in Justice."

The reports ran on. It was good for these minions to proclaim their successes to each other. First, it would provoke each one to try and outdo the rest. Second, it would reinforce the knowledge that we couldn't lose. I leant back and my thoughts drifted as the reports came rolling in. I considered the future. At some point I would have to enter that courtroom in heaven and challenge the Creator. Perhaps some practice would be useful before I hit him with the real thing. It would be uncomfortable, but not as annoying as it would be to the Creator. Such a sweet day that will be, when I present an irrefutable legal challenge to the Creator in his own court of Justice. He and everything he is, will have to come and bow before me. I will take my place in heaven and expel him. I will rule and have dominion over the whole of creation. Such a realisation must be very disturbing to him. How sad. I imagined myself, my beauty clear for all to see, sitting on the throne of heaven. There would be no more fighting or strife. Peace would reign, my way. Everyone would think and do things in my most excellent ways. No one would ever be able to threaten me again. I would be the most glorious one of all. My glory would surpass even that fading glory of the Creator himself. That would be heaven!

Egypt

Joseph! Perhaps, one of the most famous of all stories: a young man threatened with death by jealous brothers, finally sold into slavery. His brothers report it as 'death by misadventure' to his doting father. They at last are free to compete fairly for affection and are only too eager to console him in his agony at losing his favourite son. Joseph finds himself working in an Egyptian official's house, no longer the favourite son but a lowly Hebrew slave. And it gets worse. Joseph works hard. He does well. The official likes him and gives him more responsibilities. But the official's wife is a sly woman who lusts after Joseph. Trapping him she begins to undress and seduce him. But Joseph will have none of it. Eager to please God rather than the desires of his flesh he resists. The official's wife finally cracks and, realising that she will not get her way, has Joseph carried off for attempted rape. Joseph winds up in jail. Unfairly judged and condemned, no trial, only injustice.

After many years, he gets a chance. He can interpret dreams. He is allowed to interpret a dream of the Egyptian Pharaoh. Pharaoh is delighted and puts him in charge. Seven years of good harvest, followed by seven years of famine. Joseph is the second most important man in Egypt. After some time, his family are forced to come to Egypt for food. The painful story unravels and his entire family resettle in Egypt.

Generations pass and the favour of the Egyptians turns to jealousy, then to fear and hatred. The Israelites, who have grown in number from a family to a small nation, are treated as slaves, fodder for the ambitions of a material society. But still God blesses his people.

Infanticide follows. The Egyptians, desperate to destroy the Israelites, kill all their male children. But one survives. The Pharaoh's daughter takes care of him, and he is raised as an Egyptian.

Later, fleeing Egypt because of a murder, this survivor, Moses, becomes a virtual recluse in the desert. For forty years he wanders. Then God steps in and speaks to him. Quite a shock really. Moses, true to the character of Israel, attempts to make excuses and tries to worm his way out of doing what God asks. Eventually he gives in to God and agrees, he goes back to Egypt with the mission of bringing God's people out.

Pharaoh, of course, is delighted at first; after all, it gets rid of the Hebrew problem once and for all. Then he realises the economic impact of losing virtually every slave in the country and he reconsiders. After a number of 'incentives', God finally resorts to sending Death to all the firstborn of Egypt. Pharaoh concedes defeat, the economic costs of keeping the Hebrew problem became worse than the economic costs of losing them.

Again, however, Pharaoh changes his mind and chases the Israelites to the sea. The Israelites pass through the sea unharmed and the pursuing Egyptians are drowned. Although they are at last free from Egypt, the Israelites do not joyfully embrace their God and rejoice in their new-found freedom. Instead they moan and groan against their leaders and need to be dealt with rather severely.

They are given the law, a legal covenant. A nation of priests. God's chosen people to reveal his will to the world. They continually reject it and fight against God and his ways. Their rebellion loses them the right to enter their Promised Land. A whole generation is forced to stay in the desert and die before their children are allowed to enter the Promised Land.

In all of this they still seem to fail to see God's purpose. They fail to grasp the enormity of what God is trying to achieve through them. They seem painfully blind to the blessings that would be theirs if only they would obey the voice of God. Perhaps most tragic of all, they fail to recognise the law for what it is or for its purpose. It quickly becomes a legalistic list of *dos* and *don'ts* rather than a blueprint and basis for a relationship with God himself.

And so we go back to the beginning of this chapter of history and examine these events from two other points of view...

The Word

A nation was born. My chosen nation. Until now I had been working towards this goal. I now had a nation, set aside for my purposes. It was not exactly a sinless nation. In fact Israel's sins continued to pile themselves higher. However, I was to deal with the sin problem later, personally. For now, I had a new-born nation to mould. Israel was a good example of humanity. It would therefore be an excellent canvas on which to paint my picture. The history of Israel from this point onwards would be used to reveal my plan and my ways to the whole of mankind. All this in preparation for me to do my bit. Thousands of years would need to pass before I could come on the scene and every little detail would have to be in place ready for my arrival. It is true that there would be many who would continue to be deceived and still not see the truth, but this way, at least everyone would have a chance. No one would be left without the choice.

The first step in building this nation would be to demonstrate that despite their best efforts, only I could save them. In addition, it was important to establish that my will prevailed, not theirs. They considered Joseph a write off, out of the way and lost. I demonstrated that not only could I bring them back together as a family but I could save them in the process. I caused Joseph, a proud and arrogant little upstart, to be humbled. Having moulded him into a humble and forgiving man I was able to exalt him to a position of ultimate power over his family.

I then had to do the same to the family as a whole. Egypt, representative of 'The World System' or Satan's way, must be seen for what it is, dangerous and vindictive towards the people of God. So I blessed Israel. That's all I needed to do. A natural paranoia and hatred for me would prompt Satan to use his system to persecute the very people who had saved his system from destruction a few years before. I used even this to discipline rather than hurt my people. A saviour was promised, a double promise in fact. The first salvation and covenant would be of the world, a demonstration of what was to come in the spiritual. Until I arrived, in order to fulfil the spiritual side of my promises, all would be used as example and demonstration of how the spiritual laws work. I would use physical examples to demonstrate spiritual truths. All of this would provide the background and basis for my arrival.

An eternal perspective helps here. Being The Word provides me with 'the divine perspective'. This perspective is not actually difficult to understand and so I will explain. I am able to stand outside time.

This 'position' of standing outside time is standing in eternity. I am able to see the whole of history. Furthermore, because time does not exist, everything is essentially constant: in other words I do not change, everything remains as it is (or was) when it left time.

At this point, an illustration will help. Imagine you are looking at a cartoon strip. The story is told through a number of annotated pictures. You are able to see the end and the start. If you are the writer of the story, you can include yourself in the story. You are outside of the story but are able to enter it in a number of ways. You can 'speak' directly to a character, or use a character in the story to teach/lead another. You can even become a character in the story, and so become personally involved. In all of this, each picture on the cartoon represents a single point in the story and yet you still have the perspective of the entire story. You are able, by communicating with some of the characters, to reveal some of what and who you are. You can even reveal to them what they really are. You are able to reveal to them later parts of the story. You would in yourself, however, remain what you are. You are able to do different things, but you will behave 'in character' with yourself.

Here is where the illustration works. Imagine the cartoon story being the whole of history. I am you, the writer/reader. I have the ability to give my characters free will but am still able to view the entire story. I am also able to step in and change things at my will. In principle it really is quite simple. Of course, it's not that easy looking through the whole of history and giving millions of beings free will, but in principle it is simple. All of what I do is like that. Simple to understand and comprehend (so that no person is disadvantaged) but often difficult to do (in terms of will, but you all have the same 'free will').

So back to my purpose with Israel. The objective here is to use them in my story to reveal who and what I am to all the other characters in the story. This means using them (a nation) as a story within a story. A responsibility, yes, but what a privilege. It means that I am able to develop them and treat them in a different (or special) way. This did not mean that I cared any the less about others, merely that I was going to use Israel to help me reach the others.

However, dealing with individuals raises the issue of free will. Some people just don't understand how I can give them free will but still remain sovereign. Let me clear this one up as well. It is crucial to understanding my dealings with Israel. You see, because I stand outside time, I am able to give an individual free will and yet see everything that he will choose to do. Back to our cartoon strip: I can put a particular person in any situation and know how he will react and what he will choose. I can therefore prevent him getting into situations where he will 'spoil the story'. Once again, the principle is simple, but put together millions of individuals over the whole of history and it does become somewhat complex. I do (or did have or always will have) an eternity to get right though. And I am God. So you see, I can let your free will have its way and yet get the story I want. My sovereign will reigns, yet you still have free will. With me, my Dad and our Spirit anything is possible.

So we have established that being eternal provides me with certain divine qualities that give me 'an edge' over any created being (that exists in time by definition). Now my intention, of course, with man (generically I mean) was to be with him. I wanted to be his friend and for him to be mine. My intention was for us to enjoy each other. Not wanting a robot, I gave him free will, then he could choose to be with me or not. His choice. Once he made a decision, the intention was to bring him into eternity with me. Then we had a problem: mankind chose to sin. What a blow. I could not bring him into eternity with the sin there. Imagine an eternity of sin and separation from me. So where do we go from here? I had to provide a way to deal with the sin problem, and then provide a way for man to enter eternity. Of course, there would be some who would not choose to be rid of their sin. Some would choose to remain separate from me. However, for those who chose to be with me, the price was worth paying.

At this point another analogy may be worth discussing, just to clarify the state of mankind. Imagine a tree growing in an open space. Each part of the tree is a person. The tree represents the human race. Now imagine the tree without any root. It is dead. It has become wood. Now in order to save any of the tree, I need to graft some of it onto a living root. This was the plan. Israel (a branch) I would break off the tree and graft onto a living root (that's me). Some of the sub branches and leaves would choose not to be a part of the live tree. They would choose to go back to the dead one. These would then be broken off and so make space for some of the other branches in the dead tree to be grafted on to the now living tree. This process could be repeated throughout history, right to the leaves at the end of the branches (the end of time). This provides every branch or leaf on the original dead tree the option (free will) to join the live tree, or to return or stay on the dead tree.

This analogy can be taken further and indeed I will do that later, however, for now I believe it explains my purpose in choosing Israel. To me, each part of the process happens within the eternal perspective. That is, I see the final two trees, one dead one alive. And yet within time, these events happen in a particular order and for a particular purpose.

One further thing to explain before I proceed. Given the understanding of the dead tree and the live tree, you see a new perspective in my judgement and dealings with certain nations in history. If a nation or group of people is a dead branch, or just wood, it is indeed dead. If I choose therefore to use a dead stick to keep my live tree growing straight, that is my choice. Furthermore, if I choose to break and destroy or burn a particular dead branch to make room for the live tree then it should be seen in that perspective. Throughout history I have seen many attempts by man to judge me from his perspective and so get it wrong. If he would instead learn to trust that if I destroy a people or nation then I do so in righteousness. It is after all only a dead branch that has chosen to be as such, and if I choose to remove it that is my choice.

The first stage in the process was to remove a branch from the dead tree. That was to remove Israel from the world. The promised saviour in this context would physically save Israel from Egypt. He would demonstrate the spiritual dimension of salvation that I myself would come and complete. Each and every moment of Israel's history from now on could also point towards this complete salvation.

The Morning Star

"What is this promise of a saviour?" I demanded of Legalism.

"I am not sure, Your Highness," Legalism whimpered.

"Could it be the one that the Creator promised would crush my head?"

"It is possible, Your Highness."

"Then I must act immediately, to prevent this," I thought aloud.

Fear and Paranoia finally turned up and asked for my orders. "You must get these Egyptians to destroy every male child born of Israel!"

"Is genocide really required, Your Majesty?"

"You dare question my judgement, fool! Do you want to take on this coming saviour yourself, perhaps?"

"Not at this moment."

"Then do as I say. It is imperative that we prevent this 'saviour' arriving until we are absolutely ready. Who knows, we may even destroy him before he gets a chance to do anything, that would really foul things up for the Creator."

"As you say, Your Majesty."

My orders were carried out. Well, with one exception. The Pharaoh's daughter had decided to bring up one of these little Hebrew children. Well that was okay, he was being filled with my thoughts, my ways and would never be in a position to harm my purposes. Indeed this Moses might even help me.

Then came the news. Moses had lost his temper with an Egyptian that he'd seen beating a Hebrew. He had killed him. He had run away in fear from Egypt. I had lost my grip on this particular individual. Not only that, but the Creator had spoken to him personally. He was clearly not the 'saviour', since I knew that he had sinned, and as such he was under my dominion, but what was going on? What was so important to the Creator about Moses? What was the Creator up to? Moses was now heading back to Egypt with a mission, a mission from 'God', of all things. My tactics were obvious. Prevent Israel from leaving Egypt. Legalism further explained the subtleties.

"You see, Your Majesty, Moses has explained the Creator's plans to Israel."

"Yes?" I invited.

"If the Creator now fails in these plans for Israel then his Word fails."

"Indeed. Any other options?"

"Well, yes, Your Majesty," Legalism was delighted to inform me. "Any rejection of the Creator's plans by Israel will no doubt result in his great displeasure."

"Excellent, and so our plan is clear. Ensure Pharaoh keeps these pathetic Israelites worn out and low. Break their will."

It seemed so easy at first, but things did go a bit wrong. Pharaoh worked the Israelite slaves twice as hard. They grumbled and resisted Moses. Trouble was, he then came out with signs from heaven. They were easy enough to copy. There wasn't much the Creator could pull off that I couldn't and I only had to see a trick once to copy it. Pharaoh was convinced that all these heavenly signs were just tricks like those his magicians could do. True, the plagues did get bad, very bad. But I had Pharaoh where I wanted him. He wouldn't give in to the Creator, not while I could pull off similar tricks.

First Moses turned his staff into a snake. This was easy, I made all the Egyptian magicians do the same. True, Moses' snake ate up all mine. Big wow. Pharaoh was, of course, unconvinced.

Second, Moses turned the Nile into blood. For seven days the Egyptians had to dig wells to get fresh water. No problem: I copied that one too.

Next came the plague of frogs. Not difficult to copy either, but Pharaoh became concerned. In order to humour Moses and the Creator somewhat, I let Pharaoh promise to let Israel go. Moses arranged for the frogs to die. What a mess! As soon as the plague was over, it was so easy to make Pharaoh renege on his promise. There is nothing like having what you want, to make you forget your promises...

Fourth was lice. This was getting silly. Okay, so I could not get the pathetic Egyptians to reproduce this little trick. They even started howling that 'the Creator' was backing Moses. I got heavy with Pharaoh. This was turning into a battle of wills. I would not be beaten.

Fifth was flies, only this time the Creator made sure that the plague didn't affect the Israelites. Only the Egyptians were afflicted. This was getting irritating. All I could do was keep a tight grip on Pharaoh.

Next came the plague on the cattle. Once again none of the Israelite cattle were affected. My grip on Pharaoh was weakening. He was beginning to want to give in to the Creator. I had to hold on.

Seventh came the boils. A plague of boils on both man and beast. Even my Egyptian sorcerers were affected. Pharaoh was beginning to panic.

Eighth was hail, mingled with fire. Crops were destroyed and there was all sorts of devastation. This time Pharaoh cracked and again promised to let the Israelites go. As soon as Moses stopped the hail, I was able to make him see my way again and to prevent them from leaving.

Ninth was the plague of locusts. They ate every remaining crop in Egypt. Again, I lost Pharaoh and he promised to let the Israelites go. Although, once the locusts had gone I was able to reassert my control over him and make them stay.

The tenth plague was darkness. This darkness was not like anything of which even I dreamt. It lasted for three days and you could feel it. It was as if all life just ceased to be. Again, I managed to get Pharaoh to hang on.

Finally, I decided to let the Israelites go. The last plague, killing all the firstborn of Egypt, so shook Pharaoh and his people that they gave them their jewellery and gold as the Israelites left. Such a horror tactic was out of order. As the whole of Israel marched away I realised that I had failed. This would take too much explaining. A trial of strength with the Creator and it looked as though I had lost. I would send the whole Egyptian Army after Israel and massacre them to the last man. I did so. Pharaoh chased after Moses and caught him by the seashore. The sea parted and showed dry land. The Israelites passed through and Pharaoh followed. The Creator caused the sea to fall on Pharaoh and his army. This was definitely bad news. I would have to resolve this little issue with the Creator later. For now, I had face to save and blame to place. Furthermore, I needed to move on to the backup plan quickly. I had to make Israel reject the Creator.

There were many gathered around. Long faces. There was a despondent feel about the meeting. The silence was acute. They all looked to me for an explanation. I had been giving personal directions on how to direct this affair and now it looked like a complete flop. I needed someone to blame, preferably more than one. My mind raced: options, ways out, schemes, lies, they all passed through my thoughts. I had to begin.

"Today has seen completion of stage one of the project," I began. "It was necessary to allow this situation to develop in order for the trap to become fully primed. The Creator has been allowed to win this little skirmish to lead him into the snare. He will now be confident enough to reveal more of his plans to the entire nation of Israel. We shall then spring the trap. We have enough of a hold over each individual within Israel to cause them to disobey the Creator. We shall then be in a position to demand that the Creator allow us to execute judgement against them. That will be the death of Israel and the end of the Creator's plans. Victory will be ours. Vengeance will be sweet." I paused and looked around. Incredulous eyes peered back.

"You... you planned all this?" stuttered Legalism.

"Of course," I explained, "you don't for one second imagine that it took me by surprise do you?"

"Well, of course not, Your Highness." He was clearly not convinced.

"You will all soon see that my plans will come to pass exactly as I intended." I reinforced the point. "I do not make mistakes. The Creator will shortly announce his requirements of Israel. It is then that we shall pounce. In the meantime you should make every effort to ensnare each individual further."

"Your Highness," ventured Rebellion with Witchcraft by his side, "we are prepared. The groundwork is even now being laid. We shall—"

"I shall also be gaining advantage," interrupted Rejection.

"I have, of course, clearly laid out the route they can each take." Legalism was not to be upstaged.

"Enough, enough!" I silenced the developing show of one-upmanship. "Pagan, I want you to be hot on the tail of every foothold gained on each individual. However, we need a specific attack against this Moses."

"I believe I can help there," Presumption stepped forward. "I have noted that he has some weakness in areas covered by myself."

"Then you all know what to do!" I concluded. "Remember, we wait until I say before we really let loose. Until then, be subtle!"

The disgusting group broke up and scattered in all directions. I thought about my plans. This recent little trial of strength had left me tired and irritated. I knew these more developed plans would work, but I was worried. It was difficult to relax. I just wanted to get this out of the way and finished. Why couldn't the Creator just give up now? He was bound to lose anyway. It would save a lot of effort. Damn him. He was just holding out in vain hope. I would have him soon though. Just a little while longer and the universe would be mine...

"Your Majesty!" Rebellion interrupted my thoughts.

"Yes?"

"We have had our first success."

"In what way?" I half listened.

"The Israelites have been moaning ever since they left Egypt."

"So?"

"The Creator has provided everything that they have needed, but we have managed to make them moan and groan continually. They have even disobeyed clear instructions intended for their good. It not only represents a growth in my control, but it also means that we are building up the anger of Moses."

"Well done, but why are you bothering me with this now?" I inquired.

"Your Majesty, this provides a wonderful opportunity for Sickness to enter as well."

"I see, very well, go and get Sickness, Affliction and Plague. They should complement as well as help your efforts."

"Thank you, Your Majesty."

The Word

It was rather annoying. I go to the effort of planning all sorts of blessings for Israel, only to find that they rob themselves of them by disobedience. Not only that, but they surrender to wilful disobedience at every turn. It was, of course, known that this would be the case. It was not by chance that I chose them. However, it did not make their behaviour any the less annoying.

It was time to give them the Law. They wouldn't be able to keep it of course. In their current condition, they were unable to be obedient. However, the point of the Law was not to enforce good behaviour. The objective of the Law was to demonstrate or show them how sinful they were. It was also to provide a genuine guide to 'good and healthy living', that was true. But it was even more than that. The priestly activities would provide a picture of the spiritual laws and principles at work. It would be a marvellous base to build upon.

And so, the law was given to the Israelites through Moses. From simple basics to social standards, such as not killing and stealing, to complex civil liabilities about others' safety. From detailed descriptions of physical items for use in worship ceremonies, to detailed instructions on procedure at such ceremonies. Cleanliness and health rules included with dietary instructions. In fact, the Law was intended to produce a lifestyle. If that lifestyle was followed, then just as an apple falls under gravity, then blessings would fall upon the nation of Israel. Similarly, ignoring the law would inevitably bring about the curses just as drinking poison will kill.

The essence of the Law was to reveal to humanity what was just and fair. It was to draw the line between good and evil. Some philosophers might argue that where the line is drawn is irrelevant; the fact that the line is drawn is important. To some extent this is true. The absolute nature of law is harsh and cold. As time goes on, some of these laws (such as the dietary ones) may not need to be applied. Such decisions can only be made by someone with an understanding of the spiritual laws and forces that they represent. At this point, Israel had little or no knowledge of me at all and these instructions needed to be followed to the letter.

An example will serve well at this point. A baby has no understanding of fire. It may be required to keep him warm and alive. It is dangerous if touched. A parent will therefore 'draw a line' (with a safety distance) and the baby will be made to understand that to cross that line is wrong. The baby cannot understand why the fire must be there. Nor does it understand why it cannot cross the line. It knows that if it does, then discipline will follow. The parent can choose a number of different forms of discipline, but the objective of any will be to prevent the child crossing the line. Reasonable parents would not leave the baby to cross the line, roll in the fire and burn itself to death. Similarly here, the law is a set of instructions to obey, with a detailed list of penalties and disciplines which will be incurred if they are not followed. And so, the nation of Israel found itself as a baby learning a set of rules (with a safety margin) to follow and live by. The understanding to 'cross the line in order to put wood on the fire to keep it burning' would not come for some time. Such a maturity would require a great deal of spiritual growth. It is true that some individuals would receive such understanding, but as a nation, Israel would need to serve as a demonstration to all people across the whole of history. There was no hurry.

Of course, true to a baby's nature, the first thing Israel did was to disobey and try to find out where the lines were drawn. An alternative viewpoint is that they saw the lines and wanted to know what would happen if they were crossed. That is, they wanted to know how serious I was. It is interesting to reflect here on a couple of points. First, the undeniable leaning mankind has to rebel, disobey and find out what happens when they break the rules, just like a real baby. Second, the underlying trust and presumption of love on my part for them; just like a baby with its parents. Of course I love Israel, just as I love everyone in creation. That does not take away from the fact that I will discipline my creation.

Like any child, Israel did not enjoy discipline. The heart of the nation was like the hearts of its people, determined to go its own way. Some individuals did respond to my discipline but most refused. Sadly, it was necessary to wait until a new generation grew up, knowing and accepting the law. Even this new generation did not truly trust me. Even they did not try and understand. They were, however, willing to obey (in the most part). I could now at least lead them to occupy their land. They were to take possession of what I had promised to Abraham.

The Morning Star

I pondered deeply. This law was an excellent opportunity, at least, it was for me. So why had the Creator done it? Wrong and misguided he may be, but he wasn't stupid. It didn't make sense. This law just seemed to make it too easy. I must speak to Legalism, his study of each and every letter would be complete by now. It was unlikely that he would come up with any new insight that I was not aware of, but it would be worth hearing his views; after all, he wasn't entirely stupid either.

Legalism approached. He was clearly pleased with himself and was obviously going to have plenty to say. However, I was still uneasy. The Creator must have known that his law would provide us with opportunities, there was surely a reason. Was there some hidden attack that I was unaware of? I would see if Legalism could spot the sting in the tail. That would curb his smug attitude somewhat.

"Your Highness! A pleasure as always!" Legalism greeted me.

"Your findings will be of interest, I am sure," I scowled.

"The main point is this, Your Highness. The Law essentially formalises what we already know to be the case. It clarifies a few points and more clearly defines our legal rights over these humans."

"So tell me something that isn't obvious!" I pressed.

"Well, there are a couple of interesting points that could make things difficult," Legalism ventured.

"Yes?"

"There are provisions for the forgiveness of sin. It involves complex legal ceremonies, but it is there. There is now a legal way to atone for sin. Furthermore the nature of the legal penalties imposed for certain sins effectively limit our operations. In effect, the law is a double-edged sword. It provides us with new legal rights, but also clearly defines limits on our activities. The provision for forgiveness is an interesting legal point. I am as yet unconvinced of the legality of such provision."

"You mean the Creator has instigated a law that in itself may be illegal?" I was now very interested.

"Well it is possible, Your Highness. He has promised to accept the sacrifice of animals as atonement for sin. The Creator has the 'right' to decide on what he will accept in order to 'pay' for sin. However, it may be that in choosing to accept such a meagre offering, he has violated his own demands for Justice. Furthermore, such offerings, even if legally based, can only deal with the guilt of sin - they cannot by definition produce righteousness."

"I think we should consider this very carefully," I announced. "This may be the time to mount a legal challenge in heaven to the Law itself. Perhaps this is the mistake for which we have so patiently waited."

"Your Highness, I will prepare the legal arguments for you."

Legalism departed. I pondered. I prepared myself for a visit to heaven. It was not going to be pleasant. Further detailed study was essential. There would be the pain of that accursed light to put up with. It would be worth it though. When this challenge was successful, the Creator himself would be no better than me. I would have earned my way into heaven, it would be my legal right. The Throne would be mine.

I found it difficult to gather my thoughts. There was much to do. I carefully considered what the Creator's response would be. Surely he would be expecting my challenge. He would have a defence prepared. I carefully considered every option to ensure that I did not lose. To endure such discomfort would only be worth it if I won.

I was as ready and prepared as I could be. The argument was watertight. It was simple but effective. Justice demanded that the wage of sin is death. The Law provided for forgiveness of sin through the death of an animal. The law was therefore clearly unjust. Argument ends. No way out. It was clearly stated.

I approached heaven, my discomfort grew as I approached the Creator. This light was painful. Finally I was in his presence. My entire being was in agony. I fought to stay where I was, every fibre of my being straining to flee back into darkness. The pain. The pain. I gathered my thoughts. So much effort was required just to stay here. I writhed and fought. Finally I pushed the pain back. My head cleared gradually. I blocked out my feelings and senses. I regained control of myself. Then I opened myself up again, enough to communicate directly with the Creator. I could just manage the situation. I would need to get this over with quickly.

"I have been expecting you," the Creator spoke. "You have no doubt come to challenge the Righteousness of the Law?"

"Yes!" I stated.

"Then present your case."

"The law allows for the sin of a man to be atoned for by the death of an animal. An animal has far less value than a man. The law is therefore unjust."

"So it would appear," conceded the Creator.

"Such an unjust law fails to be righteous, by definition," I pressed home my advantage. "And as such the law fails. The law comes from you and since it is not righteous it shows that you are not righteous. Not being righteous you have less claim to heaven than me. I therefore demand my rightful place on the throne."

"You have not considered one thing..."

"What is that?" I inquired. How could he argue? I had forgotten nothing. The argument was self-contained.

"The demands of Justice require a sacrifice, I have promised such provision. The promise was made to Adam and Eve. Until my provision comes to pass then faith in such provision is sufficient. The law is further indication of such a sacrifice to come. Obedience to the ceremonies within the law merely express faith in that law, my provision and the sacrifice to come, they do not in themselves atone for sin. The sacrifice that I shall provide will be sufficient."

"This is outrageous!" I was furious. "First such a provision has not yet been made, therefore no atonement yet truly exists. Second, provision for such a sacrifice is based entirely on your promise, and it is your word that is in question."

"To answer your complaint on these points. Since I am eternal, then providing I do make such provision and providing the sacrifice is made, then I am entitled to view it from an eternal perspective. That means it is as valid now as it will be when it is done. One sufficient sacrifice is by definition enough. Concerning the validity of my word, you have attempted to challenge my word but have not been successful. If you can demonstrate a failed promise then your argument wins, however, you have failed to do that. My word stands unless you can bring it down. Therefore, by definition it is true."

"This is unfair!" I complained, but it was no good. His argument held. I had to prove his word had failed in order to argue that it had failed. Indeed, his eternal perspective did give him the right to look upon a future event and apply it to today. I had lost. My mind reeled.

There was no further discussion. He had maintained his argument. I was drained. My concentration lapsed momentarily and the pain came flooding back into my being. I flew away from his presence. Back to the darkness. Away from the light. The pain subsided. I was exhausted. Legalism would pay for this pain. He should have known. He should have seen this obvious defence by the Creator. I would double the workload of everyone. I would not make this mistake again.

Later, I again pondered. So the Creator was able to maintain his position providing his promises could be fulfilled. The legal approach then was still the same. His word failed if I could make any promise fail. This was getting to be hard work. He had plenty of time to bring about his promises. It was hardly fair; I had to wait until he made a move to fulfil a promise before I could stop it, or challenge it. In the meantime, all I could do was prepare the ground. The initiative was therefore with the Creator. I must regain the initiative. I wanted control of the situation. At the moment I was not in control. He had formed this nation of Israel. He was up to something. All I could do was to try and infiltrate the very 'soul' of the nation and keep them captive to me.

The Promised Land

Finally Israel was ready to enter the Promised Land. Moses, who through disobedience was unable to enter, had died. Joshua was the new leader of Israel. He was a man full of faith and obedient to God. First they entered Canaan through the river Jordan, a miracle in itself. The carriers of the Ark had to actually enter the river before God held the water back upstream and allowed the entire nation to pass through on dry ground. Once in Canaan, there were many battles to fight. There were, after all, many people living there already.

There was the battle of Jericho, perhaps the most famous battle of all but by no means the entire campaign. Rahab the prostitute helped the Israelite spies and was rewarded by being spared. The Lord gave Joshua specific instructions on how to win the battle. "March round the city once each day for six days. On the seventh day march round seven times and raise a shout." Joshua and his army obeyed. The walls of Jericho came tumbling down. The city and its occupants were completely destroyed.

The battle against the King of Ai was also won. Israel attacked and feigned retreat. While the King of Ai pursued Joshua, a second Israelite force entered and destroyed the city. This threw the King of Ai into disarray and he and his forces were destroyed. After the battle, Joshua honoured God and had the Law read to the whole of Israel.

The city of Gibeon succeeded in tricking Israel into making a peace treaty by claiming to live far away. Israel honoured the agreement and when they discovered that the city was indeed a part of the Promised Land, they forced the people to be servants.

Adonizedek, King of Jerusalem, formed a treaty with the kings of Hebron, Jarmuth, Lachish, and Eglon. Five kings of five cities with five armies, and they gathered to destroy Gibeon. The Gibeonites called upon Israel to deliver them and Joshua came to fight against the alliance. The fight was joined and Joshua began to defeat the kings. Stones fell from the sky like hail and these stones killed more of the enemy than Israel. The fighting was so hard and long that Joshua called out to God to extend the day. The sun and moon stood still for nearly twenty-four hours and this gave Joshua and his troops enough time to finish the fight. And so there was a day that was twice as long as any other, the first and only day like it ever recorded in history.

It took many years for the Israelites to fully occupy the land. One by one, all the strongholds of the enemy fell. Israel became feared among the surrounding people. Israel began to live in peace.

Once settled, however, the troubles really began. As the years went on, Israel forgot to obey the Law. In forgetting the Law and becoming disobedient to God, they were disciplined. The surrounding nations and people would cause trouble. The level of obedience that Israel showed to God was directly linked with their physical welfare, economic prosperity and political well-being. When they became disobedient, God raised up someone to help sort the problem out. God was so merciful to them. Like a father with a child, he guided, disciplined and loved this nation. And so restored, the nation's troubles were dealt with. Peace and prosperity reigned again.

The pattern repeated itself time and time again. The stories of Gideon and Samson are but two examples of the suffering of Israel amid disobedience, God intervening to help and restore, each event in Israel's history confirming the Law, confirming God's commitment to Israel despite Israel's disobedience.

The Word

This is perhaps the most bloodthirsty and warlike period in Israel's history. I often find that it is difficult to get across to humanity precisely what is so just and fair about Israel entering the land of Canaan and massacring virtually every living being in sight. Given the perspective that I have, it is obvious. However, it is not surprising that when people hear of a loving and merciful God, and then look at my instructions to Israel during this period, they become somewhat perplexed and confused.

I do not, of course, feel the need to justify my position in this matter. I mean, without wanting to appear arrogant, I am God. I can actually do as I please. However, I think it is useful and helpful to explain. To understand what is happening at this time in the history of

Israel is to understand Israel's role in history. To appreciate the loving justice being demonstrated is to begin to comprehend my holiness. To grasp the commitment to the eradication of all the enemies of Israel is to see the true spiritual battle taking place in the spiritual realm.

This is not a game. It is not a drill. I am not practising. There is no room for mutual existence. Absolute victory or absolute defeat. If you are in a dark room and the light is turned on, the darkness disappears. You cannot have light and darkness in the same place. So it is in the spiritual realm. Evil cannot coexist with holiness. One or the other.

Now apply this principle to people. They are either in darkness or light. If they choose to come into the light, then all their dark deeds and secrets will be exposed and must be removed. Once in the light, they reflect the light and so any darkness around them is also exposed.

Wherever they stand in the light there will be light and so darkness cannot stay.

In an historical context, Israel represents a light coming into the Promised Land. The other inhabitants represent the forces of darkness that have settled there. The arrival of the light means that the darkness must go. Remember that at this point, the whole of humanity is still essentially dead. To eradicate the 'dead' wood from an area in order make way for a live tree is not something that would be seen as strange. The problem is in perception. The human viewpoint sees the inhabitants of the land as being alive. The truth is that they are not only dead but also in spiritual darkness. Accepting this viewpoint and understanding it as truth is essential to realising the genuine nature of what is going on, both in history and in the spiritual realm.

So, armed with this understanding or perspective of events, we can take a closer took at some of the detail of this time. The disobedience of Moses is an excellent start. What seemed like a trivial offence incurred a costly penalty.

Each case of disobedience is sad. However lovingly I deal with it, there still has to be a certain amount of discipline. I was therefore sad that Moses could not enter the Promised Land. It was not that he himself was abandoned by me, on the contrary. However, a man in such a position was not only serving as a leader but as an example. Furthermore, his unique position also gave him unique responsibilities. His disobedience was in his use of his staff. The staff represented his authority. He was told to strike the rock in the desert and waters would flow. He obeyed, and this served as a picture of the coming promise. The rock representing me and the water, the Holy Spirit. In striking the rock he released the flow of water. This pointed to me being struck and so paying the price for sin, thus enabling the Holy Spirit to flow to all who will receive it. So far the example had worked. The problem came the next time. He was told to speak to the rock and so water would flow. The picture here being that there is no need to strike the rock (me) twice. Once would be sufficient. However, in anger Moses struck the rock a second time. This not only provided a bad example but the picture was now corrupt. Moses had misused his authority and had struck twice. This could not be corrected in terms of historical fact, but by the application of discipline the event could be shown to have been disobedience. So Moses was disqualified from entering the Promised Land. A poignant lesson. Disobedience can disqualify an individual from my promise.

Entry to the Promised Land then required obedience. Occupation of the Promised Land would need even more obedience. Continued well-being would rely on continued obedience. Simple enough. Not easy though. Once again, it is as a picture that these events in Israel's history need to be viewed. The entry into Canaan, the destruction of any previous inhabitants, and occupation of the land is a picture of the spiritual battles that will come.

In order to enter the Promised Land, Israel needed to cross an impossible physical barrier: the river Jordan, fast flowing, and at flood level. I was to perform a miracle. But rather than just stop the river and allow Israel to cross as I had done when they left Egypt, this was a good time to help them exercise a little of their own faith, obedience and commitment. The carriers of the ark therefore had to walk into the Jordan first. I then stopped the river flowing for them while Israel crossed over. Once they were over, Joshua organised an altar to be built at the place to remind them of what had happened.

Object lesson from history; when you need a miracle to cross over on dry land, obedience sometimes involves getting your feet wet. Simple really, but not easy. How do you think the twelve men felt when they carried the Ark of the Covenant into the river Jordan? I mean, there was a river that was bursting its banks and they were told to carry the most precious item Israel had into it. I mean, that takes faith and a commitment to being obedient. I know how they felt: more than a little apprehensive. They obeyed, however, and got their feet wet. Because of their obedience, the entire nation of Israel was able to pass over the river Jordan on dry land. Great stuff this faith.

The Morning Star

Abaddon (or Destruction as he is better known) approached. His dark form was preceded by Anger and Rebellion. What a team! The objective was simple. Destroy Israel as they entered and attempted to possess the land of Canaan. Legalism was already by my side and he opened the discussion.

"You do have a small problem of precedence," Legalism informed Abaddon, "the problem being that Canaan was occupied by Abraham. The land was promised to him by the Creator and as such, the people you have control of in Canaan have no legal right to be there."

"But if we can stop Israel occupying the land successfully, then surely the promise falls and we achieve our ultimate purpose as well," Abaddon responded.

"That is indeed the case," Legalism continued, "in fact, the successful destruction of Israel at this point would provide us with the ultimate legal case with which to occupy heaven."

"So you are saying that although our possession of the land is not legal," I asked, "if we maintain possession of it, then we have by default won our legal battle for possession of heaven?"

"That is so, Your Highness," Legalism explained, "I have in fact ratified the fact in advance with the Creator." His face betrayed memories of the same kind of discomfort as I had recently endured. "The possession of Canaan by Israel effectively represents the legal battle for possession of heaven."

"And you have this fact formally agreed with the Creator?" I wanted to be absolutely sure this time.

"Yes. The facts are as follows: all we have to do is maintain possession of Canaan through our human prisoners (while Israel is obedient), or cause Israel as a nation to be destroyed. Either fact, once established, hands us heaven on a plate."

"Then I have requests of you, Your Highness," Abaddon rejoined the discussion, "I wish to have all available resources and personnel at my disposal in order to achieve the complete annihilation of Israel."

"Things are not that simple." I denied the request. Such an obvious attempt to get me to surrender my authority to him was laughable. "There are a number of different methods that we must use in order to be successful. This particular approach is purely physical. Whereas victory in this area will provide us with ultimate victory, I must plan and use other approaches to ensure that we do not fail. After all, you cannot personally guarantee to me that Israel will be destroyed, can you?"

"Well obviously not, Your Highness, it is the case that we cannot see how we will fall at this time, however, personal guarantees on such matters are impossible."

"Not impossible, merely unwise. You could give me the guarantee, but should you fail you would pay, personally. This discussion has no merit. You will be provided with all the assistance you need. Efficiency demands that some resources will, however, be required on other projects."

Abaddon left with Anger and Rebellion in tow. It was strange to see Rebellion without Witchcraft. Still, they would be working together in order to destroy Israel. Legalism also departed and in due course Pagan approached. He had Religion with him. Excellent! I would brief them on their tasks.

"Pagan, welcome, I have some tasks for you and your friend Religion," I greeted them on their arrival.

"It is an honour as always," Pagan responded.

"I want you to divert Israel from obedience to the Law and worshipping the Creator, to worshipping yourself "

"A great pleasure Your Highness. But what about Religion?"

"It is very likely that such a blatant approach will not work. It will therefore be more successful if you use Religion. Religion can subtly infiltrate their minds in the guise of faithfulness. After a while, they will want more than Religion; at this point you will be able to provide the most suitable alternative to worshipping the Creator. Religion should be quite able to keep their deadened minds off the truth for long enough."

"An excellent scheme, Your Highness! Perhaps you could allow me access to Fear and Doubt as well. I have found, in experiments with other humans, that a little oppression from those two opens the door for Religion very nicely. The approach appears to be almost irresistible."

"Very well, but Destruction will also need them I am sure; you must negotiate with him for sufficient access."

Pagan left. This was excellent; we had a two-pronged attack upon Israel. One internal, the other external. They would surely fall for one or the other, if not both.

Now there was one further piece of work to put into motion. I called Deception to my attendance. He was the long term investment, the backup plan. I had a sneaking feeling that the next few years would see Israel take possession of Canaan, despite bitter opposition. The Creator was not stupid enough to let Israel be destroyed, not so quickly after admitting its legal significance. No indeed, he would be ready for the frontal assault. If it succeeded, all very good, but I suspected it would not. I therefore needed to invest in the future, perhaps long term.

Deception arrived, and we began by reviewing the work performed so far.

"You have done well to date," I allowed him a little praise. "However, we now need a planned and structured approach!"

"What do you mean?"

"Until now, you have merely attempted to copy the Creator's devices on a fairly superficial level. This will not be sufficient in future. To date, you have succeeded in copying simple tricks such as those performed in Egypt, however, we must now refine this approach."

"You have something in mind?"

"Yes. So far we only have the Word of the Creator. We need an alternative, or rather we need a number of alternatives. We need to develop lies both for short term and long term use. They must be good though, simple copying of the Creator will not fool anyone for long. We must build complex webs which are fully self-supporting."

"I see and I do indeed have a few ideas." Deception began to expand. "I have been performing my own research in this area and I would like to present some for your interest."

"Please go ahead," I listened with interest.

"Well the first is based on Unbelief, with Lies built around it to support the case. The clever bit comes when I wrap it all in Atheism, and in turn wrap that in Ignorance. The principle is quite simple; we use ignorance to feed these humans lies about their physical universe, such lies will become so entrenched in their culture that they will become a part of their understanding of the Creator. At that point, the lies can be exposed as lies, thus undermining belief in the Creator. This allows Atheism and Unbelief to enter. The result is, that any probable lie that fits the apparent facts can be used."

"Good, and has this been tried?"

"Absolutely! One of our more successful deceptions has been to trash the Creator's account of creation itself. We have managed to get people to attach all kinds of false assumptions to this, we then reveal the stupidity of some of these assumptions and their belief in the Creator's account is shattered. We have, in fact, already tried a number of approaches on this theme, all of them equally successful."

"Give me an example," I demanded.

"Well, one simple one is that the earth is at the centre of the universe. Clearly it is not, but since the creation story implies the importance of the earth, then this assumption is easy to include. We then managed to allow a few educated humans to discover that the earth goes round the sun. This crushed their perception of the Creator's Word being true and so they lost all faith and belief in him. We then used a number of lies about the origin of the world to provide an alternative explanation. Worked a treat!"

"Excellent, I want you to work on this. This will become important; the more they really discover about the universe, the more we can play this line. Begin sowing lies into every culture concerning the earth. Tell them it's flat, or something equally ridiculous. I mean it should be easy enough since from their perspective and general experience it does appear flat."

"I have more, Your Highness."

"Go on." I was intrigued, so much deception, it could only be good.

"The Law and revealed Word of the Creator, so far, provides excellent opportunities for embellishments. Remember how we did the same theme in the garden with Adam and Eve? They fall for it every time. The opportunities are endless."

"Good, anything else?"

"Yes, there is an excellent opportunity, especially for those most obedient to the Creator."

"Really and what exactly is that?"

"Money, Your Highness. The Law promises to bless obedience with prosperity. My research has found that large material wealth can be used to bring a false sense of security. Such feelings are very desirable and so money is desirable. Possession of money, especially in large quantities therefore provides power and influence. The self-perpetuating deception that material wealth provides security and control over one's destiny is therefore created. With these deceptions, we can provide the chance for many other spirits to gain a hold, such as Greed, Control and Materialism. The other offshoot is the deception that being materially well off is a sign of favouritism from the Creator. In fact, many additional possibilities lie behind the deception of wealth."

"This is all most reassuring," I commented. "I hope that you will be able to discover more uses for all three approaches you have suggested."

"I'm sure I will, Your Highness."

"Fine, remember, I want you to begin sowing the seeds for the long term as well as the short term. It is essential that we begin to solidify our grip on the whole of humanity, but especially on Israel."

Deception scurried away. A useful, if repugnant creature. Virtually all of my control over humanity was based upon his work, which was not in itself a worry, but it did leave him with a lot of power. Still, I was sure I could control him. I had ultimate legal authority over him – I was his father after all.

There was much to do and plan. Israel had become irritatingly obedient to the Creator through this new leader Joshua. They had successfully crossed into Canaan and had threatened Jericho. I marshalled all the spirits I could, to maintain control of the people in the land. The next few weeks proved to be very educational. First there was interference by the Creator at Jericho. I mean, to cause the walls to come tumbling down like that! Just because Joshua did as he was told. And using one of my spirits, Fear, to cause those under my control to melt before Israel. They were wiped out to the last man.

Fear grew as a result of that and took over many of these humans that he was supposed to leave alone. For some time, he was effectively out of control.

Witchcraft, however, had a remarkable success. He tricked Israel into making an alliance with the Gibeonites. This was a master stroke. Not only did that mean that we had permanent legal rights to settle in Canaan but it meant that we could to some extent control Israel through them. Granted, these Gibeonites were cursed and destined to stay as servants to Israel, but since I had effective control of them, then I had control of a large portion of Israel's economy.

We managed to get a bunch of kings to attack Gibeon. This forced Israel to defend them under the terms of the alliance. It should have been a whitewash, a massacre of Israel. They were tired after travelling so far, so we had the choice of battleground. It should have been easy, instead it was the other way round. The Creator was so lucky. A small oversight on my part and he managed to rain rocks on our human forces. Not only that, but by a sheer fluke of nature, the day was lengthened to allow Joshua and his forces to finish the mop up job. What luck!

There was no way he would be so lucky again, I would make sure that I had every possible factor accounted for. It was just a matter of time.

The Word

Time and timing: many human military strategists and tacticians will stress the importance of timing. Bad timing and planning can destroy a campaign before it has begun. Surprise is always a matter of good timing. In the case of the alliance of the five kings and the battle that ensued to defend Gibeon, timing was also an important factor. Many people do not appreciate the timing and accuracy required to cause those particular circumstances to occur at the appropriate time. Let me expand.

The five king alliance was essentially defeated by rocks falling from the sky. That is a meteorite storm. To arrange a meteorite storm is one thing, to calculate its arrival time is another. To ensure accuracy to within a few metres is not at all simple; after all, I had to ensure that none of the troops of Israel were hit. To arrange all that, I had to look very closely at the situation from my eternal perspective. Then I had to flip back to the beginning of time (that is creation) and ensure that as the universe was created, the required lumps of rock would meet the earth at precisely the right time.

Man thinks he's clever. He is. He has managed to put a small metal object on the moon. That takes skill and calculations. The maths involved is very delicate. I mean, one degree out in the aim and they would miss the moon and end up flying off into space. Any small error is multiplied by the quarter of a million mile journey from earth to the moon.

64

Maybe now you get the idea. I had to put a meteorite storm in place over 2000 years before and millions of miles away, aimed to strike the earth at precisely the right time and accurate to within metres. Not bad.

Then came the punchline. Joshua asks me to extend the day. I mean, stop the earth rotating temporarily; just like that. So there was another meteorite. A large one hit the earth just after Joshua prayed. The force is enough to stop the earth from rotating. Well not quite. Actually the earth's crust stopped rotating while the inside (with a liquid layer) continued spinning. Then because the inside is spinning with huge momentum and the crust was stopped, the crust gradually gets dragged along and begins to spin again. You've all seen the effect I'm sure with ice in a glass of water. Stir the water and the ice spins with it. Use the spoon to just stop the ice, allow the water to continue turning, remove the spoon again and what happens? The ice momentarily stays still but then gets dragged along by the water again. Same principle just on a different scale. Anyway, the effect to the people on the ground is that the sun stops, stands still and then moves on again. The daylight hours last longer, that is a day twice as long as any other. Simple really. It's all just a matter of timing and accuracy, although I guess being God helps.

Modern geologists have found and identified the meteorite in question. It is known that the earth suffered the impact of a huge meteorite in the Indian Ocean. Trouble is, of course, most modern scientists are such devout atheists that they never consider that their findings confirm Scripture. No, they are too busy trying to demonstrate how the facts disprove Scripture. Not that it matters too much. The truth is the truth, and I certainly do not need them. I do feel for them though. It is so sad seeing so much talent being misdirected by a spirit of unbelief. Such deception is only maintained because they do not fully understand time. They use radioactive dating techniques that are based on all sorts of false assumptions. Geological dates are mainly based on these false assumptions. But then Deception is clever. After all, if you knew you were being deceived you wouldn't be deceived, would you?

Back to the events under discussion anyway. After some time Israel took possession of Canaan. They settled. Periods of obedience and disobedience followed. I raised up judges to correct and discipline. As a nation, they allowed me to be responsible for their leadership. They grew and did well. Eventually I sent a man called Samuel. He was willing and obedient. He was one of the few in Israel in those days who could hear my voice. And so, the stage was set for a period of great significance. The next few generations were to form the foundation of the culture and background to Israel. They were to define more clearly the exact manner and purpose of me becoming a man, and so Samuel was raised not as judge, but as a prophet to Israel.

The Morning Star

"So who or what exactly is this Samuel?" I demanded.

"He appears to hear the Word of the Creator, Your Highness," Divination replied.

"And he is responsible for your recent setbacks?"

"Absolutely, Your Highness. Every word he speaks in prophecy comes to pass. The people will no longer listen to our more loyal subjects. Naturally, we occasionally get things wrong, purely as a ploy you understand, but this Samuel is always right."

"He has the respect of the whole of Israel?"

"Yes. We need a new angle of attack in order to drag Israel away from the will of the Creator."

"Very well, you are dismissed," I commanded.

This was all very interesting. The Creator was obviously up to something. A real leader was he, this Samuel? Well I had better stir up the desire for someone different. A king would be ideal, just like in the nations around them. I could gain control of the king and therefore of the nation. Perfect! What we needed here was a little Rebellion and Treachery, the ideal combination. They responded to my call and came into my presence.

"Your Highness, you have a small project for us?" they both invited.

"You are to concentrate your efforts towards making the people of Israel demand a king!" I ordered.

"Of course, Your Highness, but why?"

"Never mind why, just do as I say, you insolent pair!"

"Anybody in particular?"

"Not really, just make them demand a king. Oh, and make sure they insist that Samuel chooses him. We want to make sure that there are no legal problems once he is in place. Samuel is operating under the Creator's authority; if he chooses the king then there will be no complaints later."

"Complaints, Your Highness?"

"Just do it!"

They scurried off. This was delightful. A king for Israel. What a coup! A man, a lineage that I could control with authority over Israel. This was better than destroying Israel, to just steal the nation from under the Creator's nose.

Royalty and Empire

Samuel, a true man of God. However, Israel began to rebel. They no longer wanted to go God's way. Instead of the prophet, they wanted a king as leader. The nations around them had kings. They wanted a king. Never mind the fact that God was their king. Never mind that God had always provided for them in the past. Now they wanted a king.

God gave them what they really wanted: a strong, good-looking king, plenty of personality and charisma, but sadly no character. He wasn't a bad king, he led his armies to war and prospered. The trouble was that he was more worried about what the people wanted than about what God wanted. The people wanted a king like Saul, a king who would give them what they wanted, never mind if it wasn't right or good for them.

Soon enough though the cracks began to show. Saul disobeyed God. He offered sacrifices to God, not as he was supposed to, with Samuel, but on his own. The reason was not to please God but to appease the people. God rejected him as king but the people did not. Saul was popular with the people. Sadly, he thought that he was outside of the will of God. Later, he deliberately disobeyed God and so Samuel announced that the kingdom of Israel would be taken away from him and given to another.

This time God chose a man with a heart for God. Samuel himself was taught a lesson here. He assumed the biggest and best looking man in Jesse's family would be chosen. He called together the leaders of the town as witnesses, but he was not the one. In fact, none of Jesse's sons appeared to be the one. Then at last he was found. David, a boy not a man, busy working in the fields during all the fuss. He was anointed as king but was clearly not yet ready to take his place.

68

Saul meanwhile was in all sorts of trouble. Now given to fits of violent rage, this David was brought in to help calm him down. Through his rejection of God's ways he had opened himself up to all sorts of problems, but still he tried to keep his throne. A fearful, paranoid figurehead.

Saul and his army were busy being terrified by the Philistines and a certain Goliath.

Here is Saul the King of Israel. The leader of God's army and he is too scared to take on Goliath. So God sends his chosen leader to demonstrate his way. David, still a boy, arrives and discovers what's going on. Well the kid is shocked. He knows God and knows what he will do, so he volunteers to take on Goliath. No armour. No ranting and raving. No arguments, just one simple sling shot and Goliath is dead. The Israelite army routs the now champion-less Philistines and wins the day. David becomes a national hero, but Saul grows jealous.

Saul's fear and paranoia grew into anger and jealousy against David. Saul began to persecute David, who was eventually forced to flee for his life. Hunted and pursued by an angry king, David himself did nothing to provoke such treatment. When God offered David the opportunity to kill his enemy, David treated him as his king. David, the chosen King of Israel did nothing to assume the position. Instead he lived as an outcast from his own people.

Finally, Saul and his family were killed and David became King of Israel. The nation was united behind God's chosen king. Jerusalem became the capital of Israel and David succeeded in all his campaigns against Israel's enemies. The king prospered and the nation grew strong. David was an excellent politician. He even made plans to build a temple for God, a house for the Ark of the Covenant. Then, at the height of his career, disaster struck. He fell in love (or lust) with the wife of one of his most faithful generals. Committing adultery was one thing, but when Bathsheba fell pregnant he tried to cover his tracks. When trickery amid deceit failed to work, he finally resorted to murder and he had the husband killed.

David, true to his nature, repented when his sins were exposed. However, the damage was done. Although forgiven, he doomed Israel to war and pain for the remainder of his reign. Furthermore, his eldest child led a rebellion against him. After many years of strife and discord, Solomon became king after David's death.

Solomon was not stupid. When God asked him what he wanted, he didn't ask for riches or power, he asked for wisdom. God granted him all three. Solomon even had the honour of building the temple according to his father's plans. At the dedication of the temple, God's visible *shekana* glory entered the holy of holies, the innermost place in the temple. Peace reigned during Solomon's rule and Israel became the richest of nations. Yet despite his wisdom, Solomon married women from outside Israel. They led him astray and he followed pagan gods. He did not remain faithful to the Lord.

The Word

Sometimes Israel could be very tiresome. They had wanted a king. It really wasn't a good idea. All a king could do was distract them from my purposes. There really was no way that it would do any good. They wanted a king though, and Samuel was upset, he took it as a personal insult. For a moment, he failed to realise that it was me they were rejecting and not him.

There was another problem. Choosing to have a king was second best, that was a fact. In addition to that, they would want a very 'macho' king. Forget about someone who would do what was right and just, someone who would follow my ways. They wanted a man with charisma. Well my Dad and I talked it over and decided that the best approach would be to give them what they wanted. Then, when it all turned to tears, we would give them a king of our choice. The Holy Spirit agreed. To be fair though, the Holy Spirit would need to come upon their choice of king. He would, of course, reject our ways but he had to be given an equal chance.

It is true that the end result would be Israel with a king of my choice, but even that was not ideal. The ideal was to have no king. However, they had to be allowed to exercise their free will.

Samuel anointed Saul. The Holy Spirit came upon him and he prophesied: he became their king. Now they had their much cherished leader. Saul was a real personality and the people loved him. Unfortunately, personality and charisma are no use without character. Despite this, I was with him in all that he did, at least to begin with. Later, he rejected me and my ways.

The problem here is that it is not right to force the Holy Spirit upon someone. If they are determined to reject the leading of my Spirit, what can I do? I could, it is true, overrule him, but that would be the same as taking away his free will. There is, of course, another side to this. The Holy Spirit is a person, yes indeed, like me he has feelings. He will only enter and lead another person as far as he is allowed. Let me explain further so that you can understand.

Each person is made in the image of God and this means that each person has a body, a mind (or soul) and a spirit. The image here is I (Son) equal body, mind equals Father, and spirit equals Holy Spirit. Now, add to this a horizontal division of the mind, that is, the will, the emotions and the intellect. In this way we can build up a picture of a person in his entirety. However, we know that the spirit of man is dead. Adam and Eve saw to that when they sinned. Their spirit died. Now the way man was supposed to work, was for the spirit to lead the mind and for the mind to govern the body. However, since the fall (that is the sin of Adam in Eden) the spirit is dead, and sure enough the body follows the spirit and dies after some time. The body, or flesh, is continually fighting against this, since it does not want to die. Hence we have the situation where the flesh is in charge. Sometimes people are ruled or led by their flesh, sometimes by their mind. Be it emotions or intellect, but in every case you will notice that the will has fallen subject to something since the spirit is dead.

There is one other possibility. Given the fact that people have a dead spirit they have a 'spirit-shaped hole' in their being. They are not complete until this is filled. They can choose to leave it empty and be led by their flesh or emotions or intellect. The other choice is to allow a spirit to enter them and to be led by that. This is the crunch, which spirit will they choose? It could be a spirit of Lies or Destruction or Jealousy or whatever evil consumes them. It can be the Holy Spirit. Once a person has opened themselves up to a spirit (whatever sort) it tends to grow within them and occupy more 'space'. This space must always be full. So the choice continues, Holy Spirit or otherwise. If a person continues to be filled with the Holy Spirit then all is fine. However, if they begin to reject the Holy Spirit and refuse him entry, then they begin to leave a gap. This gap will be filled. You see, the Holy Spirit is a gentleman, he will not invade, he will only occupy where he is given permission. Not so with evil spirits. They will often exercise a legal right to occupy but without gaining the individual's consent first. Now here we have a problem. What happens when the Holy Spirit meets an evil spirit? Well, it all depends on the individual. If he allows the Holy Spirit to enter, then the light expels the darkness and the evil leaves. However, if an individual shuts the Holy Spirit out of an area then darkness takes over. The choice stays with the individual.

Now let us consider one further thing. It is my Dad who sends the Holy Spirit. The way to him and hence the way to receive the Holy Spirit is through me, no other way will do. All you do by going through any other route is open yourself up to an evil spirit masquerading as the Holy Spirit. So before I came, physically, people had to have faith in the promise and so get to the Father through me. The principle was still the same. The Holy Spirit was available to people before I came. Similarly, people also rejected him.

So it was with Saul. A man of good looks, great personality and physically strong. He relied on and followed his flesh. When anointed as king over Israel, the Holy Spirit also came upon him as he allowed. Later, he rejected the Holy Spirit and in so doing opened the way for all manner of evil to consume him. It started with Fear, Fear of the people and what they would think, and so the downhill slide began. Once full of the Holy Spirit, he emptied himself of it and chose rather to be full of evil.

It was at this juncture that my Dad and I knew that he had made his choice, and sadly, the Holy Spirit, now grieved by his displacement, withdrew entirely from him. We instructed Samuel to anoint David. This was in fact highly amusing. Samuel was still looking at the flesh, although, hearing from my Spirit, was somewhat surprised at our choice of David. But here was a young man of character, open to the Holy Spirit, continually filling himself, he knew me and loved me better than anyone in Israel at the time. His heart was on fire for my Dad and the anointing as king was really just a ceremony. He was already full of the Spirit.

The Morning Star

Things were going better than planned. Fear arrived and gave his report. Legalism was as usual in attendance for an in-depth analysis of events.

"Your Highness, I have much good news."

"Yes?" I enquired.

"Saul has completely rejected the Creator's Spirit and so left himself wide open to us. I have personally managed to gain a

72

complete grip on his thinking. We have, in effect, control of the King of Israel."

"Has the Creator's Spirit been completely eradicated?" I was delighted.

"He has in fact withdrawn completely, Your Highness. Our superior power was clearly too much for him to endure."

"But what of this report I have concerning Samuel's rejection of Saul as king?" I wanted to know more about this.

"Your Highness," Legalism explained, "Samuel has prophesied that the kingdom will be wrenched from Saul and given to another."

"And who is this other?" I demanded.

"David, a shepherd, not much more than a boy. He has no legal claim to the throne and yet Samuel has anointed him. Such stupid actions being done in the Creator's name imply some kind of trickery."

"What do you think, Fear?" I asked.

"It is true that David has no chance of ever becoming king, so I conclude some form of trickery."

"There is no need for concern," I announced. "I already have War and Conquest controlling the Philistines. They have a champion, Goliath. With Fear in Israel's heart and the Philistines around, we will crush this Israel completely. This pathetic David will also fall by the sword."

Some time passed and I heard that David was called to soothe Saul's mind. The more we took control of him, the more symptoms of rage and paranoia gripped him. Excellent. The heart of Israel was melting. But David was a different matter; whenever he played his music it seemed to calm the king. It seemed that somehow the Creator's Spirit was able to calm Saul through David. I was unsure and unhappy about this. This David would have to go.

Finally I set up the challenge between the Philistines and Israel. Goliath taunted the entire army of Israel. This was fun. As the final dregs of courage melted from the hearts of the army of Israel, I prepared the Philistines to move in and annihilate Israel. Then this David arrived, I watched carefully. The Creator's Spirit was definitely upon this boy. It was actually uncomfortable to be near him, the presence of the Creator shone so strongly from within him. Instead of choosing armour and heavy weapons, he chose to fight Goliath with a puny sling. I watched as this pathetic boy approached the most mighty warrior of the time, I relished the moment that was to come. This example of the Creator's way was about to be snuffed out like a candle, the Philistines would massacre Israel. Then my relish and delight slowly turned to horror as the events unfolded before my eyes. This puny David shouted to Goliath; he came against him in the name of the Creator. The Spirit within him shone painfully and it was almost impossible to see in the brightness. At that moment, a single sling shot hit Goliath in the head and down he went. It all happened so quickly, Fear suddenly lost his grip on Israel as they allowed this same Spirit to fill their hearts and soon there was an army of light coming against the Philistines. A riot followed.

This was almost a disaster. It certainly stopped the imminent destruction of Israel. The only redeeming fact was that Jealousy had slipped into Saul's heart. I now instigated a methodical persecution of David. Through Saul, I tried to pin down David and kill him. If he was to save Israel then he had to be destroyed. Every attempt failed. Instead, each time I got Saul close enough to perhaps attack, David by pure chance got the opportunity to kill Saul first. Each time he spared Saul's life and Saul went back home full of remorse.

I continued to use the surrounding nations to attack Israel. During one of these battles, Saul got himself killed. I still had not managed to destroy David and now he came to Israel where the tribe of Judah pronounced him king. Descendants of Saul were still around and I used them to contest David's claim to the throne. I incited civil war against David within Israel and began to sow the seeds of division within the nation, Judah on one side and the other tribes (Israel) on the other. The situation deteriorated, however, when David finally reunited both Judah and Israel under himself and made Jerusalem his capital. I called a meeting of minds in order to bring this 'godly king' down from his throne.

"We are gathered to assess the current situation and develop plans for David's downfall," I announced to the numerous attendees, "There must be a concerted plan of action in order to destroy his household and all respect for him. His death would be ideal. Let there be no mistake; the destruction of Israel is the prime objective. At this time, however, it seems that a military approach is unwise. We must therefore follow the path of destruction from within."

Legalism reviewed the present status, "Currently, there are a number of outstanding promises due to mankind, Israel, and David.

These promises become more specific as they apply closer to individuals. It is therefore logical that causing a promise to an individual to fail will cause the failure of the more general promises. Such an event will provide us with the opportunities required to finally oust the Creator from heaven and so resume our rightful place. So, specifically concerning David, the Creator has made the following significant promises:

There will always be a descendant of David on the throne of Israel. One of his descendants will rescue his people from their sins.

This means that the downfall of David becomes crucial to our plans. The destruction of the tribe of Judah will in effect be the destruction of Israel, much more so if Israel themselves bring it about.

Having examined the facts carefully, a personal attack on David is most likely to be successful. There is, I believe, an ideal approach in this direction?"

"Indeed," all heads turned towards Lust and Adultery in surprise. "We have examined the subject carefully and discovered that the one area that he leaves unguarded in his heart is associated with sexual immorality. Whereas he has not broken any laws as yet concerning this, we are confident that he can be drawn into sin on this matter."

"But what of the Creator's Spirit?" I inquired. "Does he not fill himself with it every day and so exclude your entry?"

"Absolutely," they both chorused. "However, he has many concubines who have weakened his resistance to our influence. He has excluded this Spirit of Light from this area in his life and as such we have been able to gain a foothold."

"Well done, please continue..."

"Once we have drawn him into sin, then I am confident that he will surrender easily to Deception in order to cover his sin. He is so used to walking so openly before the Creator that any sin will devastate him and it will be possible to drive him into all sorts of trouble in order to cover it. We have consulted with Murder and although he has been careful to ensure that there is no innocent blood on his hands, he still does have the ability to admit Murder."

"An excellent proposal," I agreed. "You shall implement it at once. We will open a Pandora's box from within his heart and he shall fall like a stone. This pit we have ready for him will overwhelm him. We will keep him and his kingdom ensnared."

The meeting finished and the plans were put into action. The execution was a delight to watch, Bathsheba bathed naked in full view of the palace. David called her to him. She willingly complied and Adultery took a hold. She fell pregnant (that's what I call timing) and David felt forced to cover his tracks. Deception offered him an easy way out and he fell for it. He called Uriah (Bathsheba's husband) back from war and tried to entice him to sleep with his wife. Uriah, however, (we left him well alone) honoured his fellows at the front line and refused to go home to his wife. David was sunk. At this point, **Murder** offered him a final solution and he took it. Uriah was deliberately left alone in the thick of the fighting on the front line. He was killed. David took Bathsheba to be his wife and thought he had got away with it. Meanwhile Adultery, Deception and Murder lay deep in his heart, threatening to consume him in darkness just like Saul.

I called another meeting to plan how we could best press home our advantage on this matter. There was no way he was going to survive this. I was jubilant. Victory was within our grasp. This David was finished!

"An excellent operation!" I congratulated Lust and Adultery for their plan and execution.

"Unfortunately, Your Highness, there has been a setback." Deception volunteered the bad news.

"What do you mean?" I demanded.

"We have all been displaced again," Deception continued. "The Creator's Spirit challenged David through Nathan the prophet and he repented. He voluntarily surrendered himself to be cleansed of the matter and in the face of such light we could not stay. All of us, Murder, myself, Adultery and Lust were thrown out with the most terrifying violence by the Creator's Spirit. It would have been possible for us to hold on, except that David has accepted the salvation of God. He has put his faith in the saviour to come, promised by the Creator. He has therefore the ability or right to receive the Spirit of the Creator whenever it moves upon him. Moreover, it was able to fill his whole being despite his sin. It was a great shock. We had not been challenged in this way before and it was impossible to stand against. The Spirit entered on the basis of the forgiveness of sin and its removal. Until now, we had only had to contend with sin been covered and we have therefore been able to hold on. This was something new."

"This is indeed serious." I was now very concerned. "Legalism, what is the story here?"

"Your Highness," Legalism began, "I have examined this matter carefully. As you know, although the law allowed for forgiveness of sin, the soul of all individuals still seemed to retain any sin committed. The act of sacrifice covered the sin but it still remained in their memory. This enabled any hold we had to be maintained, although sometimes weakly. This is indeed a new phenomenon. David has managed, through faith, to receive the forgiveness promised. He has, through his understanding of the Creator and his close walk with him, grasped the truth of the promise. He has managed to reach into eternity and place his sin on to God's promised provision. In so doing, his personal sin is not only dealt with, but also removed from him. He has broken through the sin barrier and is now as close, if not closer to the Creator than before."

"And this is legal?" I was incredulous.

"Provided the Creator provides and fulfils his promise to remove the sin legally, then anyone can do this. This is indeed legal. The Creator has promised to forgive and deal with sin. Faith in that provision means that legally, any human being can be free of sin."

"If the mere exercising of faith enables a believer to receive this forgiveness, the removal of sin, and then to be filled with the Creator's Spirit, then it means trouble. This must not become common knowledge." I was now very concerned.

"Indeed, Your Highness, fortunately such understanding is very rare. Furthermore, we can apply the full weight of the law to all individuals who do not receive such forgiveness."

"So where does this leave us?"

"The Creator has pronounced certain punishments against David for his sin. We will be allowed to maintain war both inside and outside to Israel for the rest of his life. Absolom his son is greedy and full of bitterness; we can create civil war through him."

"So you are saying that apart from a few individuals, this forgiveness thing can be kept under wraps?"

"Yes, Your Majesty."

"And we can continue to sow strife and disaster upon Israel?"

"Yes, Your Majesty."

"Then to war!" I declared. "We shall split this Israel in two and cause the nation to fight against itself. We shall make every attempt to sow the seeds of destruction and disobedience in every king that rules. And we shall wait and be prepared for this coming provision of the Creator. Clearly, everything hinges on the success or failure of a single individual yet to be born. I suspect that I know how this must happen. I shall consider this matter more carefully. In the meantime, sow as much destruction as you can..."

The meeting was adjourned. I sat back and tried to think. Everything tied back to this promise of salvation. There was no way that any human would ever be able to save himself. So how was this salvation to come? It would need the sacrifice of a perfect human being, yet none could ever exist. I had the entire family of Adam under my power – they all had sin. So how was the Creator going to try and provide this perfect human? It just didn't make sense. And yet there it was, the promise. The whole future of humanity and for that matter my future depended on how the Creator was going to fulfil this promise. Or at least, how he was going to try...

The Prophets

After the death of Solomon, the kingdom again became divided: Israel and Judah. Each had a separate king and, in the line of kings for each kingdom, some were good and some were bad. During these times, God sent prophets to prophesy against or for the various leaders, the most famous examples of which are probably Elijah and Elisha. They were around during the reign of Ahab, King of Israel.

Ahab was an evil man. His wife Jezebel practised witchcraft openly and they both worshipped Baal. His sins brought trouble to Israel. God sent Elijah to pronounce the start of judgement against him. Elijah announced that because of Ahab's sin there would be a drought throughout the land. Then he turned and left. He went away from civilisation and from the influence of Ahab to a small stream called Kerith Brook. Here he had water to drink and he was fed each day by ravens. Eventually, the severity of the drought even caused Kerith Brook to dry up and so he headed north.

Elijah stayed with a widow and her son. The widow had only enough food for one last meal. When Elijah asked her to feed him she objected and explained how she and her son were about to eat what was left and then starve. Elijah insisted and the widow, recognising him as a man of God, submitted to him and baked bread for the three of them. They ate together. To her surprise she noted that there was still just enough food for one more meal. Each day the same thing happened. She would use the flour and oil to make bread, but there would always be sufficient for one more meal. The widow was encouraged and delighted that God was providing for both her and her son through Elijah.

Then disaster struck; the son died. The widow verbally attacked Elijah and demanded to know why God had done such a thing. Elijah remained calm. He went upstairs to where the body lay and prayed. He had the same question to ask (rather than demand) of God. Led by the Spirit, he lay on top of the boy and prayed further. Slowly, the boy returned to life and perfect health. He returned the lad to his mother.

Then, after a long stay, Elijah departed and went to Mount Carmel. He sent word to Ahab and all Israel to gather there with the prophets of Baal. A challenge was set. The god who answered with fire was God. They would each build an altar, place wood and a bull on it, and pray. The god whose sacrifice was accepted with fire would be deemed the true God. Elijah challenged Israel to look and choose that day who they would serve, God or Baal.

The prophets of Baal went first and they made their altar. They danced and prayed, they cut themselves to gain Baal's favour. Nothing happened. Elijah taunted and mocked them. Eventually they gave up and it was Elijah's turn. He built an altar, placed the wood and bull on it, and dug a trench around it. He then proceeded to soak it in water. So much water that it filled the ditch surrounding the altar. Then Elijah prayed. As soon as he did, fire fell from heaven and consumed the lot, including the water.

Israel as a nation turned back to God. They chased and killed the prophets of Baal. Ahab mounted his chariot and sped back to Jerusalem. Elijah prayed for rain and the clouds gathered. He then ran back to Jerusalem himself, overtaking Ahab in his chariot. Then it rained, well, it poured.

Jezebel, not one to give up so easily, plotted to kill Elijah. When Elijah heard, he panicked and in fear of his life ran away to the Sinai desert. There he collapsed. Later he awoke and sat depressed and despondent, feeling all alone, without a friend in the world and weak with hunger. Angels came to Elijah and fed him. Then God encouraged and helped him, pointing out that there were still people in Israel who had not turned to follow Baal. Refreshed and restored by God, he went back to Israel and nominated his successor, Elisha.

Years of training followed, after which Elijah was taken up to heaven by God in a chariot. Elisha saw it all and so received from God what was promised; a double share of the Spirit that had rested on Elijah. Elisha had been a good and faithful servant of Elijah and was now ready to take his place. To start with, Elisha just went home.

Elisha and his servant looked like they were in big trouble. An enemy of Israel had been losing battles and discovered that it was because Elisha could tell the commanders of Israel's army exactly what their battle plans were. So, the enemy decided to kill Elisha. A whole army headed for Elisha's home. They camped outside and prepared to kill him. Concerned, the servant reported this fact to Elisha, suggesting that they run for it, or hide, or do something. Elisha responded by pointing out that there were many more on his side than there were with the enemy. The servant was confused and so Elisha prayed that he might see. Suddenly, the servant got a glimpse into the spiritual world and the truth of the situation. He could suddenly see thousands of angels encamped around them too. The enemy were themselves surrounded and hopelessly outnumbered. Just as the enemy prepared to come down and take Elisha, the army of angels struck the troops blind. Just as the confusion reached its climax, Elisha strode out and led the entire army to the Israelite garrison. So, from an earthly viewpoint, Elisha captured an entire army single-handed.

The Word

As expected, things went downhill in Israel very quickly. Solomon's empire and economic influence had made Israel into a great power. His unfaithfulness to me sowed the seeds of destruction. The divided kingdom was in tatters, Israel and Judah each selfishly followed their own king instead of following the law I had given them. A succession of evil kings had virtually wiped out any trace of loyalty to me. It was sad to see a once great nation being brought to ruin by its own rebellion. It was time to demonstrate once again that evil cannot triumph.

Causing a drought may be considered harsh, but suffering can help focus people's minds on what is really important. It does at least serve to polarise opinion; it produces decision. It doesn't in itself make people turn away from sin, but it does help to force a decision about which way to go. This was the case here. Elijah went and informed Ahab about the drought. However, the response was not repentance but a willingness to do even more evil. The people suffered and all that happened was that whatever side of the fence they were on, mine or Baal's, they stayed there, although most of the people couldn't make up their minds. They would flit between me and Baal. The suffering helped to concentrate their minds. They were ready to make a decision.

I have to say that I love the truth but I also love to win, I am a winner; I never lose, I am, after all, God. To offer a challenge to Satan, like the one at Mount Carmel may give the impression that I was just showing off. In a sense, that impression is true; I was just showing off, but the underlying purpose was not for me to show off how strong I am. I don't need to show that I'm strong or a winner as I am. I don't need to show off to anybody. In this case, the purpose was to show the truth and thus the people of Israel could decide who they wanted to follow or what they wanted to do. In order to allow them to make a fair decision, I just had to ensure that they got to see the truth. The purpose of the display of power was therefore to enable Israel to make a decision, I was not just showing off. The time came for Baal to answer with fire. Pagan and Satan were busy readying themselves to cause the sacrifice to burn up. However, I had a team of angels on the spot, ensuring that it didn't happen. When Elijah started mocking the prophets of Baal, I must say, I had a little giggle. Perhaps he's on the toilet! Well, Satan was certainly straining, but not in that way. Finally they gave up, and Elijah prepared his sacrifice. Timing was perfect. Bet you can guess how I did this one after the 'Joshua longest day' story. Anyway, fire and fire and fire. Precision aiming, precision timing. Down from heaven on to the altar. Bang! The whole lot, gone.

The Morning Star

I finally wrestled free of the angel. One last swipe and he was sent tumbling through space. I looked around; the troops had done well. Within seconds every one of us was free. Angels flying off in all directions. Pagan approached me. He looked battered and weary. His thick hide was covered in cuts and bruises, evidence of the recent fight. There was a crimson flow above his eye, obscuring what would be a deep scar.

"The Host of Heaven, Your Highness," he panted, "we have succeeded in seeing them off. However we were unable to respond to the pleas of the humans, such was the ferocity of the fight."

"Any casualties?" I asked.

"Not this time. It was close though. A number of scarred and wounded," his thick heavy breath swirled about.

"Listen to me!" I called to all those present. "All of you can now bear witness to our strength. The Host of Heaven just attacked us.

Unprovoked, they had surprise on their side and yet we still won! Some of you suffered some minor scratches, but not one of you is really hurt and there are no casualties. Does anyone see any trace of the Host of Heaven?"

"No!" came the resounding shout.

"Indeed," I continued, "they have fled, in fear of our superior might and strength. Victory is ours!"

At that moment Elijah's prayer began. Then silence, Fire fell from above and consumed his sacrifice. The presence of the Creator's Spirit could be felt. It moved in on all the humans present. With all my troops busy regrouping after the fight, these humans responded as one to this new move of the Creator: they turned on the prophets of Baal, my worshippers.

Again, Elijah prayed, I looked round. What the hell this time? I was having a bad day. The storm clouds gathered and for the first time in years it began to rain upon Israel. I grabbed Witchcraft and dispatched him to find Jezebel. She must destroy this Elijah. Ahab headed back for Jerusalem while I watched this man of God, Elijah, run straight past him. The Creator was certainly flexing his muscles today.

Elisha, trained by Elijah, was causing more trouble than Elijah himself. I had a king with enormous resources, committed to the destruction of Israel but each time he drew up battle plans, God explained them to Elisha. Elisha told the Israelites and the plans failed. He had to go; I was determined to get rid of this Elisha even if I had to use the entire army to do it. So I did. I got my people to reveal to the king the cause of the problem. They headed for Elisha's place, army and all. Next morning, they prepared themselves to go down and get him. This time we were prepared. Suddenly, every man in the army was struck blind. I leapt up to see what the problem was - The Host of Heaven again! Before I could gather the troops Elisha was leading the army off into captivity. This was happening too often but I felt impotent to stop it. Something needed to be done.

Wisdom, Song, Poetry and Prophecy

Despite his unfaithfulness to God, Solomon did have great wisdom. Much of his wisdom was captured in the form of proverbs and songs. His father David had written many songs of praise and worship, as well as prayers recorded as psalms. Other such writings include prophecies and parables. Many of these works were given during the tumultuous period of history following Solomon's reign. Some of them, within the context of this writing, need some special mention.

The Song of Solomon, or *Song of Songs* is the 'blue' book of the Bible. It describes the love and passion that a man and woman can have for each other, in a context that is not only blessed, but pleasing to God. Sex outside marriage is strictly prohibited by the Law. However, the union of man and woman within the marriage covenant is not just allowed, but intended. Marriage is indeed a covenant. The total commitment of a man and a woman to each other. *The Song of Solomon* is explicit in its description of the passions and feelings of two lovers. It details some of the sexual act and the joy it can bring. These descriptions are given in a manner that allows the reader to understand the love and tenderness required while not filling the mind with perverted and lustful images.

Job was a man with a problem. Although upright and righteous in all that he did, he did have a problem. He didn't quite trust God. He was scared for his family. When Satan was allowed to curse him with poverty, he only blessed God. When Satan was allowed to take his family and incite him through his wife, he continued to bless God. But when he himself was struck with illness and his friends smugly accused him of a lack of integrity, he himself questioned God. He failed to have God's perspective and assuming his own righteousness he questioned God's justice. God was not pleased and put Job firmly in his place. Job repented of his presumption and so God blessed Job

with another family. What was more, he blessed Job with double the
material wealth he had before. God's Justice of paying back double
what was stolen was fulfilled. Satan was not happy.

Jonah was another man with a problem. He was a prophet who
loved Israel but hated every other race. He failed to understand that
although God loved Israel, it didn't mean that God hated everyone
else. It meant that God wanted to express his love for the whole of
mankind through Israel. Jonah didn't want any part of that. Blessing
Israel was okay, but helping out the gentiles? You could forget it. So
when God told Jonah to go and warn the people of Ninevah (gentiles)
he thought to himself, why should he go and warn them? If he
refused, they would continue in their wicked ways and God would
destroy them. In an effort to try and get away from God, he got on a
boat and left Israel. But soon he realised that there was nowhere to
run from God. Jonah ended up being disciplined by God by being
thrown overboard and swallowed by a huge fish. In the depth of
darkness he cried out to God and repented, saying that he would go
and warn Ninevah. After three days he was vomited out onshore near
Ninevah. He proceeded to warn Ninevah of the coming judgement of
God. Disappointingly for Jonah, the king and subjects of Ninevah
repented and God relented, not sending the destruction he had
threatened. Jonah sulked in the hot sun because these lower forms of
life had been spared, just as he knew they would be, God used a tree
to teach Jonah the lesson that he needed to learn: God loves everyone.
Some are chosen to do certain things, some are chosen to reveal his
love, but he loves them all, everyone.

The Word

Marriage is a covenant. A covenant is more than just a contract.
A contract is a legal commitment by two parties to do something for
each other. A covenant is an understanding that each party will do
whatever is needed by the other. A contract includes details
concerning the basis on which the contract can be terminated. A
covenant is valid for the lifetime of the parties. A contract has
penalties and opt out clauses in case of failure to deliver. A covenant
can assume delivery will take place. A contract is based on mistrust
of the other party. A covenant is based on trust.

It is a fact that throughout history, the marriage covenant has often
been treated as a contract that can be terminated. This is not what

was originally intended. In fact, the marriage covenant, between a man and a woman was meant to be a picture of the relationship that I was to have with humanity. Unfortunately, the picture has become cloudy and unclear, marred by the perception of marriage.

My commitment to mankind is complete and unreserved. I chose to enter into a covenant with man. Despite him continually breaking the various covenants so formed, I persevered and put all that I am into preserving the covenant. Soon the time would come for a new covenant, one that people could keep, but until then the picture of marriage would have to suffice.

Sexual relationships are intimate. They represent the joining of two people on the physical level. This type of intimacy and commitment is only possible within the marriage covenant. Such a joining of two parties is indeed joyful and pleasurable, but it requires commitment on both parts to keep it that way. Marriage in this context is representative of my relationship with mankind. I do expect and require man to be faithful to me – how would you feel if your partner was unfaithful? I will not let go of people who commit themselves to me – there is no 'divorce' option. There can be no real joy or meaning to my relationship with people until they are committed to me in covenant – no sex before marriage.

I am happy and joyful that so many marriages are the way I intended and do provide a reasonable picture of how I want to relate to mankind. I am sad that so many people destroy the real joy intended for them by becoming involved in sex before (or outside) of marriage, or surrendering to the injustice of divorce.

Job was a good guy. I mean, he was great. But I had to deal with that lack of trust and that Fear. Satan was only too willing to help; he didn't realise it, of course, but he was going to help. I knew of his plans (nothing is hidden from me) and I decided to allow him enough rope to hang himself. Then I would use the events as they unfolded to heal Job's fear as well as bless him more abundantly. Until this time, I had posted angels around Job and all that he owned. They were a protective shield against evil, ensuring that no harm came to him. I do that for those that follow me.

The angels were in procession before me in heaven. Then, like an injured animal, Satan came into my presence. It was a sight. The creature that wanted to take over heaven, cowering in pain merely because he was in my proximity.

"Satan!" I called, "Where have you been? What have you been up to?"

"Oh, roaming to and fro down on the earth."

"Have you seen Job?" I asked. "He's one of the good guys."

"Yes, but would he be if you allowed me to take everything that he has, so that he is reduced to nothing? I'll wager that he would hate you then."

"I think not, but you may test him."

So Satan bounced off in glee, while I commanded the angelic shield to stand back temporarily. He struck down Job's wealth. He killed his children. He destroyed Job's home. He even persuaded Job's wife to incite Job against me. Job was firm.

Satan came back to heaven and we had a rerun of the above conversation, only this time Satan wanted to afflict Job's health. The same story. Job became ill with boils all over his body and bad breath. His wife incited him to curse me and die. Job was resolute. He continued to praise my name.

Then Job's 'friends' came along. I use the word loosely. With 'friends' like that you hardly need enemies. Instead of simply having compassion for the fellow, they verbally beat him up. They accused him of all sorts of things just to satisfy their own desires to see their perception of justice. Job tried to defend himself, but could not convince them of his integrity. Pity they didn't bother to ask me my opinion! Anyway, Job had finally had enough. Convinced that he had done nothing wrong, he questioned me and my justice. The cheek! Here I am, helping him, by dealing with the problem of Fear who has got a hold on him and he dares to question my integrity, because he is so sure of his own. Well, after giving him a good rap across the knuckles and helping him to see things in perspective, he realises that he has spoken out of turn. Now, instead of Fear, he learns to have respect for me. We got there in the end. To finish with, I bless him with double what Satan stole from him. The same number of children (he will still have the others in heaven), and twice the wealth. Satan may be mean and nasty, but he is very firmly on a leash and anything I allow him to do is for the good of my people.

Jonah, dear Jonah! He loved being a prophet but he just didn't understand me. He couldn't quite grasp how much I loved him. He was therefore unable to understand how I could love others. Perhaps more importantly, he was unable to love others himself. I found just the project for him. It would release him to be loved and love others, and at the same time, it would save an entire city of people: Ninevah. A hotbed of violence, sexual abuse and injustice, not a good man among them. So I sent Jonah there to warn them that if they didn't change their ways, I would level the city.

Jonah was not happy. He thought that running in the opposite direction would cause the people of Ninevah to continue in their ways. That would mean that I would execute judgement against them. How wrong; he failed to grasp the concept that I never execute judgement without first warning. It is true that not everyone receives or listens to the warning (that's their choice) but I always ensure that one is sent to them.

So, Jonah had to be disciplined before he delivered my warning. That provided the opportunity for my Spirit to waken their conscience and so they repented. The city was saved. Jonah was still unhappy. I had to explain that I loved them as much as I loved him. I loved him enough to have mercy when he disobeyed and so I would have mercy on Ninevah too. Finally he got the message. Once Jonah received and understood my love for him, he was set free to be joyful when I loved others. I do enjoy releasing people.

The Morning Star

Marriage. Pathetic! What a picture. I would need to ruin this example. Family units and values? There was no way that I could allow this sort of stuff to propagate. Divorce, injustice and strife. That's what was needed. Indeed, it would provide a much better background for us to infiltrate young children's minds. Why, we could even get the parents to abuse the children. I was well aware that these humans often saw the Creator in a similar light to the way they saw their parents. What an opportunity to discredit him then. I called together a meeting.

"The very fabric of society must be attacked," I announced. "Full impact on the family unit. I want to see Adultery and Divorce at every possible opportunity. If we can break the back of these family units, then we can stop the children being open to the Creator. Their perception of him will be distorted and so make it easier for us to gain control!"

"An excellent policy, Your Highness!" enthused Legalism. "The legal consequences of such sins can be inflicted up to ten generations

88

later, too. It has, since the Law, become possible to attack these humans without them even knowing how we gained the legal entry. They are completely blind."

"A delight," offered Guilt. "Such sexual enterprises always enable me to enter. Abuse of such a gift from the Creator gives me the ideal legal entry. And once present, I can bury myself behind all sorts of reasoning and excuse. But I get a hold and I am able to call in other attacks continually."

"And it is so easy," Lust spoke. "Many of these people have no self-control and so either surrender to me or to Religion. Both myself and Religion then often make space for Perversion to enter."

"This type of strategy must be pursued at every level of society, in every land, and for every human. Most concentrated efforts must be made in the areas and families where the Creator's Spirit is present." I concluded the discussion. "You may go and begin."

They left me alone. I turned my thoughts to Job. It was annoying having such a goody two shoes around. It might even be worth a visit to heaven to make this one fall...

I had argued the legal case well. The Creator had been forced to concede. I destroyed everything Job had. All that was precious to him, I took. The cursed creature still refused to curse the Creator though. I would have another go.

Deep glee and satisfaction – I could send Sickness upon him. No sooner had I done that than I incited him, through his wife, to have a go at the Creator. It was no good; he was too stubborn. His friends did a good job for me though. They managed to get him to challenge the Creator's integrity by lifting up his own. Laugh? I absolutely howled in delight. Unfortunately, my glee was short-lived. The Creator stepped in and corrected Job. Then, he posted an even bigger guard around Job. Job received many more blessings than he had done before. Still, at least I had proved that not a righteous man had or ever would live.

Ninevah was a triumph of my policies. There was so much sexual immorality there, it was a joke. It just proved that the strategy worked. I had complete control of the place. With the lessons we had learned in taking control so effectively, it would for ever be an example of how to destroy society. Excellent. Then disaster; the Creator intervened. This bloke Jonah turns up after all, despite my best attempts to prevent him and warns Ninevah that the Creator is about to flatten the city. The fools actually take some notice and there was that Spirit of the Creator again. They stopped what they were doing and asked him to spare them and what's worse is that he did. Ninevah turned into a prime example of what happens when people repent. Still, we had learned the lessons that we needed to learn.

My attention finally turned to all these prophecies concerning the coming saviour and the end times. The Creator was certainly sticking his neck out here – very specific. This saviour would not be difficult to spot, and it was going to be the Word himself. What a coup! The Creator himself in human form. No glory, no protection, no dazzling painful light. He would become an easy target and all this specific prophecy about him. All I had to do was manoeuvre him into breaking one letter of the law, or failing to fulfil one dot of prophecy and he would be finished. Killing him would be the easiest way. Failing that, there would be plenty of opportunity to put him under enormous pressure.

However, some of these prophecies did bother me. They also described my destiny a little too well. I didn't like that. What the Hell though, I only had to ensure that the Creator failed on one little crossing of a 't' in the entire law and prophecy and I could claim his failure. None of his prophecy need come true and I could take my rightful place on the throne of heaven.

Legalism and I studied these scriptures carefully. It would not be long now. Daniel had even announced the exact arrival time of this promised 'Messiah'.

A Saviour Is Born

The first Christmas; Jesus born in a dirty stable and laid in tight clothes to keep him warm and placed in an animal's feeding trough. Full of fleas – what a way to enter the world. Forget the images conjured up by *Away In A Manger*, being born into a filthy stable full of animals like that is not pleasant. It was cold, full of germs and noisy.

The shepherds come and go, the Magi arrive and leave their presents. Herod hatches a plot to kill every child in the area (just the same tactics as Pharaoh of Egypt, but that is no surprise; the same guy was behind both of them).

Joseph takes Mary and Jesus to Egypt to protect them from Herod. They stay there until Jesus is a young boy. On their return to Nazareth the family is welcomed. Still, Jesus carries the stigma of an illegitimate child. Despite all the prophecies and pronouncements concerning Jesus, in Nazareth they just don't care, they think that they know better.

Jesus grows and learns his trade as a carpenter. He leaves his parents and makes his own home. At last the time for the beginning of his ministry began. He goes to be baptised by John the Baptist in obedience to a call from his father. The Spirit comes upon him and he is led into the desert. After some forty days of fasting, Jesus is weak and hungry. Satan chooses this time to come and tempt him.

The Word

Dad, the Spirit and I were together, as one. I knew what was to come and we prepared ourselves for it. It was necessary. It was the only way, I agreed. I was willing and so the great battle was begun; the decisive battle. I was to go to earth, I was to become a man and I would need to trust Dad like I'd never trusted him before.

In order to legally enter the earth, I would have to be born. I would therefore have to be conceived. I would have to grow, be born and live through childhood. I would have to become a human. I did not relish the thought. My only access to Dad would be through the Spirit. I would have to lay aside my glory in order to become human. I would be entering time and I would, for some thirty or so years, be human and experience humanity in real terms. I would be exposed to all the risks and concerns to which mankind was exposed. I would become vulnerable and would have to rely on my human parents.

The Spirit came upon my mother to be, and Mary conceived. At that precise moment in time I became totally human. My mind went blank. Every fibre of my being screamed to be back with my Dad. I felt conscious but oblivious to everything. I was not entirely sure of anything for some time...

The time had come for me to begin. I went to my cousin John. It took some persuading, but he finally agreed to baptise me. Once done, the Spirit came upon me. I heard my Dad say how pleased he was. Immediately, the Spirit led me to go and fast in the desert. I followed the Spirit's direction. Day after day went by. I continued to pray and talk with my Dad. I spent time with the Spirit. I had to learn how to hear him clearly. It was not easy, in this human body there were many distractions. My body craved to be satisfied. I allowed my spirit to lead, and the voice and power of my spirit grew stronger within me.

Many days passed and I learned to respond to the slightest lead of the Spirit. I learned to be as close to my Dad through the Spirit as I was when I had been in heaven with him. Until now, I knew that Satan had been held back, prevented from directly challenging me, but now this was to change. Very soon I would feel the full onslaught of his deceptions. In this human frame it would not be easy. Not only was the future of humanity at stake, but the whole of eternity. If I failed, then the very throne of heaven would fail. This was how serious the situation was. For the next few years, I would minister and disciple some close friends. Then I would face the ultimate test. Right at this moment, however, I must prepare myself for the battle to begin.

I stumbled over some rocks. My body was weak and craving food. The heat was intense. My mind was flooded with strange thoughts. What if all this was just my imagination? What if God

92

didn't really exist? How could I possibly be God? Such foolishness.
Did I really think that I was going to save humanity? A voice of
reason spoke. I heard it quite clearly.

"If you are God, the Son of God that is, turn these stones into
bread," the voice said. Quite right, I thought. So obvious. In so
doing I could prove to myself that I was who I thought I was.
Furthermore it would be doing the sensible thing. I could eat the
bread and so prevent myself from collapsing. What a good idea! I
was pleased to have thought such a thing. But wait. Had I thought
that? I paused. My Spirit stirred and indicated that it was foolishness
and vanity to do such a thing. It didn't make sense, I thought. I
chose to obey the Spirit, rather than the voice of reason. The
scriptures came to mind,

"Man shall not live by bread alone," I said.

Immediately I found myself standing on top of the temple. I
looked down. It's strange isn't it, that at the best of times if you look
down from a height, the compulsion to jump really is enormous. In
this case, it was everything I could do just to stop myself from falling,
never mind to jump. My legs felt weak, my eyes were heavy.

"Just relax and fall. God has said that if you fall he will command
the angels to save you so that you will not strike the rocks below."
The thought and reassurance went through my mind. Yes, it would be
so nice. Just relax and that would be it. The angels would catch me
and I could sleep. Somehow it wasn't right though. It was Scripture
for sure, but something was wrong. Somehow this was not good. I
just knew it,

"Do not put the Lord thy God to the test," I allowed my Spirit to
say through me.

I could see the whole world, everything, every kingdom, every
person and every land. A warm friendly voice made me an offer:

"I will give you dominion over all this, just bow before me." Well
it made sense. I mean he showed me the legal documentation to show
that he was prince of this world, all I would have to do would be to
bow to him. Seemed reasonable. I would then have authority over
the whole world and would have achieved my purpose. Again, the
Spirit stirred within me:

"Thou shalt have no other Gods before me." I refused to comply.
I would worship God, my Dad only.

I felt the comfort and power of the Spirit come upon me. Angels came and fed me. I relaxed and thought. So clever, this Satan was smart; the subtleties of the deception in each case! Now I could think straight, I could see the lies hidden behind the words: the first, an attempt to make me confess self-doubt and abuse my authority; the second, an attempt to make me presume upon my Dad; the third, an offer of something that isn't even his – the earth and everything in it belongs to the Lord. There was Satan offering what was mine to me. Subtle. He was a sharp operator. I had not even seen the deceptions; thankfully the Spirit was able to lead me on the correct path. I must not forget these lessons. I cannot trust my own understanding. I must always submit to the leading of my Spirit.

The Morning Star

The gathering was large. The opportunity had come and gone. There would be others, but there must be no mistakes. Everything was at stake now. This Jesus was a tough nut to crack. He was just too good. I had nothing against him... yet.

"There will be other opportunities," I announced to the collection of vile creatures present, "we must not fail. There will be a number of avenues through which we can attack but first I want to hear some of your thoughts on the matter."

"A difficult case, Your Highness," Legalism spoke softly. "I have managed to establish without a doubt that this is the one spoken of... all indications point to him being The Word."

"The Word," I quizzed. "The Word himself, as human, how can this be?"

"Your Highness," Legalism continued. "He has legally entered the world through this rather messy birth and childhood process. Most irritating, but there it is. I have investigated the matter most thoroughly and every fact points to the same conclusion: He is the fulfilment of the prophecies; He is so far without sin; He is The Word."

"So this is not just some jumped up prophet," I sneered. "The Word himself, as human. How delightful!"

"Just so Your Highness!" Legalism agreed, there were snickers of delight from the others.

"Then our strategy would appear obvious," I stated logically, "the same methods of attack as we have tried previously, but applied to him specifically. We must try and lead him to sin in any way possible. Also, any failure to fulfil what is prophesied about him will be adequate. His death would be ideal. I do, however, have some concerns that we must address and understand; currently he is without sin, and so that makes him different. Legalism, tell us the implications."

"Your Highness," Legalism began, "It is difficult to define fully, since he also holds the authority of the Creator, and the Creator's Spirit seems to operate in great power wherever he is. This much is for sure, however, he is as a man like Adam before Adam fell into our hands. We have no authority over him. There may be some legal tricks we can use, but I suspect that they will not be watertight. However, he does have legal authority over us. He has no power in his own right, only authority."

"Please explain, for the benefit of those present, precisely the difference," I commanded.

"Authority is the legal right to command," Legalism explained. "He has authority to tell us what to do, but no power to make us do it. That is, we can refuse to submit to his authority. However, the Spirit which never leaves him has the power, but no authority. That is, the power cannot operate without authority. Imagine the Spirit as a tank in a battle; it has the power to destroy all the infantry. A man has the authority to kill but no weapon. That is Jesus. However, when they work together, the man, Jesus, has the authority, and the tank, the Spirit, has the power. Together they can push us around. In summary, while he operates within the confines of the Spirit, he has both authority and power. He is in control."

"Thank you," I granted Legalism. "Has anyone any personal experience of this?"

"Your Highness," Infirmity and Sickness chorused, "he throws us out of people on a regular basis. We have no strength when he is around. He just commands it and we feel compelled to obey. Not that I would want to stay around him; his very presence makes me want to run a mile."

"Then our approach must be subtle," I concluded. "We must try and make him operate without the Spirit. That, in itself, will fulfil all that we require. In addition we must destroy him."

I was unhappy. This Jesus, The Word was, in effect, the greatest opportunity and yet he was seemingly so perfect. It was relatively easy to prevent most of the leaders in Israel from accepting him, but he continued to wreck many parts of my kingdom. Everywhere he went, light poured into people's lives and he set them free. Years of work was being undone in seconds. He had to be stopped. If this continued, he would end up setting the whole world free.

It was some three years later and I had finally managed to manoeuvre things into place. Jesus had upset a number of the religious leaders – they were so easy to manipulate. A few rumours and stories, a little pressure on them personally, threats about losing power. and they considered Jesus their worst enemy. They were determined to kill him. The people as a whole, however, loved him, they thought he was great. I knew how fickle such people could be, especially with a little external pressure. And that was exactly what I had planned. Jesus would have a choice: come up with a few miracles when he shouldn't, or have the crowd turn against him. He was in a corner. Just a few more days and I would take complete control of Judas and I would then have him prisoner.

"Your Highness, we have an emergency!" Death burst into my presence.

"What is it this time?" I snarled, angry at being disturbed yet again.

"Jesus has released someone from my grasp!"

"So what?" I demanded. "He has been releasing people all over the place, you will just have to take your victim later."

"But Your Highness, I think you misunderstand, I had already taken this Lazarus. I had him for three days!"

"What?"

"He was already dead, he didn't slip out of my hands. I had him. Dead and buried. In the grave. Three days. Jesus came along and just called him forth. Lazarus just got up and walked. He broke through my power like a knife through butter."

"I see," I responded and thought for a few moments, "I think this matters not. We know that he has such authority and power. Soon he himself will be captured by you. Then he will be silenced for ever."

"I see, Your Highness." Death seemed to remain doubtful.

"Just accept what I say. Once we have this Jesus killed, all our worries will be over. How can he set people free once he's dead? We will have him under our power. He's finished."

I sat and wondered. Something about all this disturbed me. I hadn't rested properly for years. I just knew I was forgetting something. Something was wrong, but what could be wrong? Once The Word was dead, he would be unable to do anything and so by definition he would fail in his appointed task of saving anyone. We would be able to move back in on all those he had released. The throne of heaven would fall and it would all be over. I would be God.

Death of A Hero

Guilty. Jesus was tried and found guilty. Of all the charges that were brought against him, the only one that stuck was that he claimed to be equal with God. Quite a claim. The Pharisees and Saducees were convinced. They didn't believe him, thus he was guilty of blasphemy, of the worst kind. He must die.

Unfortunately, they did not have the authority to put him to death; that was up to the Romans. Pilate would do as they asked. He just wanted a quiet life and with the amount of noise they were about to make, he would be forced to do what they wanted.

Jesus was sentenced to death by crucifixion. Barrabas, a liar and murderer, was set free. Pilate did not really want to kill Jesus, since he could find no basis for the penalty and had in effect pronounced him innocent. He tried to release him under the terms of an agreement whereby he released a prisoner every year at this time but the crowd had cried for Barrabas and he was left holding Jesus, a very hot potato indeed. Pilate, in an attempt to pacify the frenzied crowd, had Jesus flogged. No good; they still cried for his blood. Eventually Pilate gave in and commanded that he should be crucified.

Nails were driven through his feet and hands into wood. The wood was raised up for all to see. Two thieves and Jesus. All three hanging on crosses. A cruel and sadistic method of killing. Jesus said a few words as the agony went on. Each and every word fulfilled Scripture and prophecy concerning himself. Then, amid a darkness that seemed to cover the entire land, he died.

Later they checked him to see if he was dead. It was surprising that he had died so quickly. Normally, they broke the legs of crucifixion victims so that they died quickly of asphyxiation. With Jesus, it was not needed; he was already dead. They forced a spear into his side and blood and water flowed out. As any modern doctor knows, the separation of the blood into blood and water only happens after death. He was dead. They took him down and buried him in a tomb. Jesus was dead and buried.

The Word

We had just eaten the Passover supper, I knew what was to come. I really didn't want it. The twelve and I gathered in Gethsemane to rest. I went off to pray. I was almost pleading actually. I didn't want to die, especially not like this. It was going to be bad, I mean really bad. Every time I took my desire to Dad he sadly said no. It was the only way, this was why I had come. My primary reason for being born was to die in this way. I had agreed to it, I knew he was right. He just seemed so far away and here I was about to face it all, on my own.

It was still the middle of the night. Judas returned with the temple guards and he pointed me out. The other disciples, so desperate to avoid the obvious, began to fight. I called a halt. One of the temple guards had lost an ear in the scuffle. I reached up and healed it. He was no more guilty than the rest. I was arrested and the disciples deserted me. Scared and concerned for their own skins, I was on my own. They brought me to trial, if it could be called a trial. These people were so full of hatred and fear, combined with jealousy and rage. This wasn't a trial, it was a lynch mob. Of course, all their charges failed and finally they demanded of me if I was God. Well, what could I do? I had to tell the truth. That was it, no pause to consider if I might actually be telling the truth, they just assumed I must be lying. As such, their demands for my death were understandable, if unfair. I was beaten, mocked, flogged and nailed to a tree.

The physical pain was one thing. Actually, after a while the body goes into such shock, that the pain becomes a dull ache. You are aware that you are really hurt, but somehow you don't feel it completely. No, what is worse is the reason for it and the reaction of everyone around. Pure hatred. To be totally rejected by everyone was pain indeed. I had loved and cared for these people. I had even healed some of them but not one helped, not one spoke for me, not one comforted me. As I hung there, looking down, all they could do was cry for themselves. None of them cared for me. I prayed and asked Dad to forgive them all; they didn't really understand.

The time drew on and darkness fell across the land. The Spirit began to withdraw from me. I called out to Dad. Why was he leaving me? His face turned away from me. The Spirit left. Darkness poured into my soul. Sickness and Disease filled my body. I writhed in a new and fresh agony. Fear gripped my heart. My whole being wanted to scream but could not. All the filth and sin of every age fell upon me. Darkness and blackness. Cold stark terror. Every nightmare became reality. Every pain was magnified. I fell. I fell. I fell. Death's icy grip took a hold. I willingly gave myself over to him. Like a vice around me, he crushed my very being. I sank and sank, into the very depths of Hell...

The Morning Star

"I have him, Your Highness," Death burst in followed by a myriad of demons squabbling in delight.

"So soon?" I inquired, pleased.

"Yes indeed, he was easy, he just gave up."

"Excellent." I could hardly contain my relief. There was a chorus of delight from the throng. This was good news. I continued, "Well done, all of you. We have now secured our position here on earth. I must add, that we will, I believe, be in a position to take the throne of heaven very shortly. Legalism will provide us with a detailed report."

"Your Highness," Legalism began. "May I first congratulate you on such an astounding success. I must say, that I did have reservations as to the feasibility of this particular venture, however you have proved your point. Legally, I see the position as follows: The Word is now under our power. He has failed to complete all that he was meant to do. As the Messiah prophesied, he was meant to establish the kingdom of the Creator on earth and it can be clearly seen that he has failed to do that. Finally, we have a watertight legal case. The Creator's Word has failed."

"Shame!" I mocked sarcastically. "Poor Jesus! Poor Creator! They're finished, all washed up. Now we can gather together our papers and go and have some fun in heaven."

Much fun and partying began. This was great. Time for celebrations...

Legalism rushed into the party with Death. I was half-cut. It is amazing how intoxicating power is, and to be free to taunt Jesus was the best. I was almost out of it.

"Your Highness, Your Highness," Legalism called and prodded at the extremities of my presence. Slowly, I regained some form of clear thought.

"What is it?" I moaned, peering at them. "You look very serious."

"We may have a problem," Legalism attempted to break through into my clouded, intoxicated mind.

"Forget it!" I brushed them away and continued my fun...

Legalism and Death stood before me. I was unhappy, to say the least. My head was still spinning but I had come down with a bump. I was angry and fed up with being disturbed. What problem could there be that was so important?

"Something is going on Your Highness," Legalism explained, "the curtain in front of the holy of holies in the temple has been torn in two. This seems to represent that the way to the Creator is now open to anyone."

"And there's more," spouted Death, "I have lost my grip on a number of the dead. A large number of people have just got up and been released from my power. I cannot seem to hold them."

"I hear you, but I am very unsure of what you both mean or of the significance." My mind was spinning. What was I to do? "Where do we go from here?"

"The situation appears to be somewhat out of control," Legalism continued. "Heaven itself is quaking. I am expecting some mighty move of the Creator at any moment."

"What can he do?"

"Well, nothing I believe, but I do have one small concern."

"Yes?" I was now very irritated.

"Well, it has to do with the legality of Death here holding Jesus."

"What?"

"Your Highness, it is possible that it is illegal."

"Explain yourself and be quick!" I felt the cold panic spread through my being.

"Well, when he died he was still without sin."

"How can that be?"

"We never succeeded in making him sin, Your Majesty."

"But he was covered in the stuff when I saw him in the grave!"

"Precisely, Your Highness, but it wasn't his. It was the sin of humanity. That is how Death lost his grip on so many. Their sins were removed and so he lost power over them."

"Okay, so Jesus has all this sin so we at least have him."

"But, Your Majesty, I suspect there will be something else to come."

"This is unacceptable," I stated emphatically, "I want you to work until you can give me a definitive report. Cancel the party. Everyone is to return to their posts. Let's get this thing settled."

Death and Legalism departed. I scowled to myself. It couldn't go wrong now. It just couldn't! I had him in my hands. Jesus was dead. The Word was in my power. I couldn't lose him now...

Epilogue

Easter morning. The very first. Jesus has risen from death, alive. At first, his disciples, still shattered by his death, were unbelieving. Then, as he continued to appear to them they believed. He continued to teach and instruct them, he showed how clearly the scriptures had prophesied his death and resurrection. Finally, before he ascended back to heaven, he told them to stay in Jerusalem.

Pentecost. The Holy Spirit is poured out over the disciples. Once scared and fearful they now had, living inside them, the same spirit that had lived in Jesus. Peter preached to crowds and told them all about the resurrection. The disciples themselves began to perform miracles, just like Jesus.

Saul, a Pharisee, was extremely zealous for the law and persecuted the disciples. But then on the road to Damascus, Jesus revealed himself through his Spirit and Saul became a disciple. Now called Paul he went on to spread the word to the gentiles.

A new church was being built. Anyone who accepted Jesus as their saviour immediately had access to the Holy Spirit. The Holy Spirit would come upon them, all they had to do was ask. A new age had begun.

The Word

Three days passed. Three days of Hell, I mean *Hell*. The entire sin of mankind was on me and I had descended into Hell. Now the sin was left there. The job was done. Every demon that exists tried to keep me there but they hadn't enough power. The power of my Dad surged into my being. Demons grappled and Satan himself hung on to me, the harder they fought the greater the power that flooded into me from heaven. The pressure was terrific and something had to give - they did; Death, Satan, Hell and every available demon. All together they strained to hold me. They failed. I burst upwards and rose from death. Life surged into my body. Nothing could contain the power that surged through me. My Dad had come through. I was alive!

The Morning Star

Disaster! Total and utter disaster. There we were when the Creator's voice boomed from heaven.

"On what grounds do you hold my son?" the Creator called.

"He has sin," I responded.

"He has no sin of his own!"

"True, but he has the sin of humanity." I was very concerned, Legalism was advising me and I was not at all convinced we had a case.

"That was put upon him as he died. You do not, however, have any right to keep him."

"Then what becomes of the sin?" I inquired.

"It was on earth, now it has been carried by his death to Hell, there it can stay. Jesus himself did not deserve to die!"

I paused. So this was the sting in the tail. He was going to leave the sin with me and expect me to calmly hand over his son. No way. I was unsure about the legal grounds I had but I would think of something.

"I disagree," I responded finally. "Jesus is dead, in death he will stay!"

The heavens shook. This was it, a showdown of power. Every demon stood alert and ready, each one primed for this moment. We would hold this Jesus in Death, I would not let him go. The heavens opened, the spirit of the Creator moved, to where I was not sure, but I could sense the disgusting holiness that was its nature. Jesus himself stirred. My minions held him down. I could feel power flooding into the soul of Jesus. His presence began to feel like being in heaven; the light, the pain. We held on. We fought. The brightness grew. The pain intensified. Never before or since have I experienced anything like it. I hung on in agony. Death gripped Jesus like a vice. The brightness continued to shine. Blinded and dazed we all hung on. I would not let him go.

The light had gone. The pain receded. I examined our position. Curses. Jesus was gone. We had failed to hold him.

We immediately began a containment exercise. It was vital that this did not continue. People on earth were beginning to believe, especially the disciples. I started rumours of stolen bodies; I had stop this spreading. The Pharisees and Saducees were, of course, only too willing to help cover up. When word that Jesus had risen from the dead reached them, they began persecuting all who even spoke of such a thing.

A few weeks later Legalism approached with more bad news.

"Your Highness," he began, "the disciples have received power from above."

"What do you mean?" I asked.

"The Creator's Spirit has come upon them and resides in each of them."

"Oh no! Can we contain it?"

"They each behave with the same courage and wisdom as Jesus himself. It is as if every believer was Jesus. We can contain them by killing and imprisoning them but more and more keep appearing all the time. It is as if a new light is turned on every few minutes. It's horrible!"

"But what of Saul, wasn't he adamant about destroying them all?"

"Your Highness, he too has become one of them. He shines brighter than the rest. We tried to kill him but failed. This is worse than Jesus himself. It's like having hundreds of him running about."

"Very well, we must develop a plan to destroy this new phenomenon. It will be simple. Discredit their stories, kill them. We will destroy these Christians!"

The Word

I ascended back into heaven and sat by my Dad. I now understood people even better, I was able to help my Dad direct operations for people's benefit. Everyone who believed in me could receive my Spirit. As they learned to obey his voice and submit to my Dad's authority so they grew stronger. The power of the Spirit grew within them. Some of them would do even greater works than I had during my ministry. Every one of them was a saint.

Dad could look upon them all with favour. The sin problem had been dealt with, salvation had been provided. Each and every person could receive blessing from God. I could look upon every situation and talk to my Dad about how best to solve it. Whenever required, I could send my Spirit to help and comfort those in need.

Satan was a defeated enemy. He still chose to fight on. Indeed, he was to put into action some of the most horrible plans against my people but the ultimate battle had been won. It was done. The final battle was still to come, it was true, but the war had been decided.

And so, my root was planted. Dead branches were grafted on to the root and they came alive. As the living sap rose through the tree, each branch burst into life. The spring sunshine shone on the leaves. Blossom appeared. Fruit formed and grew. Truly a tree of delight. Some branches refused to bear fruit and so were chopped off and replaced. More dead branches were grafted on in their place. They too came alive and grew. The harvest would indeed be plentiful.